Iroquois Stories

Heroes and Heroines
Monsters and Magic

Other Books by Joseph Bruchac

Indian Mountain and Other Poems, 1971, Ithaca House, Ithaca, N.Y.

The Poetry of Pop, 1973, Dustbooks Press, Paradise, Ca

Flow, 1974, Cold Mountain Press, Austin, Tx.

The Road to Black Mountain, 1976, Thorpe Springs Press, Berkeley, Ca.

This Earth Is A Drum, 1977, Cold Mountain Press, Austin, Tx.

Entering Onondaga, Cold Mountain Press, Austin, Tx.

The Dreams of Jessie Brown, Cold Mountain Press, Austin, Tx.

There Are No Trees in The Prison, 1978, Blackberry Press, Brunswick, Maine.

Mu'ndu Wi Go, Mohegan Poems, 1978, Blue Cloud Quarterly, Marvin, S.D.

The Good Message of Handsome Lake, 1979, Unicorn Press, Greensboro, N.C.

How to Start and Sustain A Literary Magazine, 1980, Provision House, Austin, Tx.

Translator's Son, 1981, Cross Cultural Communications Press

Remembering The Dawn, 1983, Blue Cloud Quarterly, Marvin, S.D.

Children's Books

Turkey Brother and Other Tales, Iroquois Folk Stories, 1975, The Crossing Press

Stone Giants and Flying Heads, Adventure Stories of The Iroquois, 1978, The Crossing Press

The Wind Eagle and Other Abenaki Stories, 1984, Bowman Books, Greenfield Center, N.Y.

Iroquois Stories

Heroes and Heroines
Monsters and Magic

As told by Joseph Bruchac

illustrated by Daniel Burgevin

The Crossing Press
Trumansburg, New York 14886

Some of these stories appeared in earlier collections of Iroquois stories, *Turkey Brother and Other Tales*, and *Stone Giants and Flying Heads, Adventure Stories of The Iroquois*.

Thanks to the following publications where the following stories first appeared:

Parabola for "The Two-Headed Snake"

Cricket for "Rabbit and Fox" and "How Buzzard Got His Feathers"

The Barkeater for "Four Iroquois Hunters"

Text copyright © 1985 by Joseph Bruchac
Illustrations copyright © 1985 by Daniel Burgevin
Cover designed by Betsy Bayley
Text designed by M.J. Waters and Wendy Skinner
Typesetting by M.J. Waters

Printed in the U.S.A.

Library of Congress Cataloging in Publication Data

Bruchac, Joseph, 1942-
   Iroquois stories.

    1. Iroquois Indians--Legends. 2. Indians of North America--Legends. I. Title.
E99.I7B85 1985   398.2'08997   85-5705
ISBN 0-89594-167-8

Contents

Introduction

I. Telling the Stories

It is more than fifteen years now since I first began telling stories. Though I had heard stories since childhood, it was not until our own sons were born that I began telling them to others. A few years later, Elaine Gill of The Crossing Press asked if I ever told any stories which might make a good book for children. That was when I began putting my versions of these Iroquois folk stories down on paper.

As I said in the introduction to my first collection of Iroquois tales, *Turkey Brother*, all of these stories are much older than my own voice. They are from the traditions of the People of the Long House, the Haudenausaunee. Though these are my own versions, they are based on originals which existed long ago, long before the first Europeans came to this earth on Turtle's back. Further, other versions of all of these tales have been previously published by various ethnologists and writers—some of whom, such as J.N.B. Hewitt, Arthur Parker, Ray Fadden, David Cusick and Jesse Cornplanter, were themselves of Iroquois ancestry. None of these stories are written down here for the first time. I have been fortunate enough to hear some stories which, I believe, have yet to be "recorded," but I am neither an ethnologist nor a folklorist, only a teller of tales. I have been told by many Native American people that it is right that I have not tried to disclose things, to tell stories which were not meant to be told, tales which are special and sacred.

Arthur Parker, the foremost collector of Iroquois legends, once described the various ways in which Indian stories have been told. These were "poetic" retellings which bury the story in fine flowery language, "fictionalized" retellings which change plots, situations and names to make things work better, tellings by "amateurs" who betray their unfamiliarity with the material by working in foreign allusions and inconsistent elements, "sectarian" tellings which point out the foolishness of native belief when compared to biblical teachings, "philological" versions which are painstakingly literal (and unreadable) word for word transcriptions and, lastly, Parker's own "folkloristic" approach in which the story maintains its form and sequence, its spirit and original consistency, but is set forth in fluent English. My own method of retellings has been closest to the last of these, but with one difference. After having learned a story—usually by a combination of hearing a version of the tale told to me and then going back and thoroughly researching all the written versions of that tale—I have tried to internalize it, to make it a part of me. I've brought to it my own familiarity with Native American people and Iroquois culture—as it is today, as it probably was long ago—and then, without notes or a written text to follow, I've told the story aloud. My aim has been to rediscover the oral quality of each tale. When I have finally reached the stage of writing down my own version of a story it has only been after telling that story aloud many times. Since I've told most of the stories first to my own children, I have judged the effectiveness of the tales by their responses and, later, by the responses of other audiences—both Indian and non-Indian, both children and adults.

I learned storytelling from a number of people—usually without knowing that I was learning anything. My own grandparents should be mentioned first. Though my grandfather didn't tell traditional Indian tales, I can still hear the stories he used to tell as he sat in front of the general store he ran for more than 40 years. His is one of the voices which strengthens my own. Later, in my young adult years, I was fortunate enough to have several teachers whose reputations as great storytellers were well-deserved. One of those teachers was Swift Eagle, an Apache-Pueblo who labored for many years in the Adirondack tourist attraction called *Frontier Town* to show people a different kind of Indian than the hostile savage of movie cliches. It was not an easy job, but I remember both his patience and his laughter. His album from Caedmon "The Pueblo Indians in Story, Song and Dance" (TC1327) is a model for me of the storytelling voice, a voice which does not hurry, a voice which speaks each word slowly, clearly, and as it should be spoken. Another mentor has been Ray Fadden, Tehenetorens. A major force in the revitalization of traditional Mohawk culture and pride in their Iroquois heritage, he has always been ready to show how good stories are teachers bearing lessons of the right ways to live in balance on this earth. His Six Nations Indian Museum in Onchiota,

New York (just north of Saranac Lake) contains more about the Iroquois people in its few rooms than most major public museums. I also cannot speak of storytellers and teachers without mentioning Dewasentah, Alice Papineau. Head Clan Mother at Onondaga; her house has been a little United Nations for many decades. I know of few people as gentle and as firm as Dewasentah in her devotion to the old ways. While I was doing storytelling and poetry with the students at the Onondaga Indian School three years ago she gave me two gifts which I treasure. One was a small lacrosse stick with an eagle plume attached to it. The other is a name which I try to be worthy of—Gah-neh-goh-he-yoh. It means "The Good Mind."

I also cannot forget another of my teachers—the land I've been fortunate to live on throughout most of my life. My wife Carol, our sons Jim and Jesse and I live in the house I was raised in, a house built by my grandfather on the foundation of another house owned by my great-grandparents before it was destroyed in a fire. The house is on land which was once farmed and hunted by the Mohawk people. Indian corn grew and still grows here. Nearby Saratoga Springs was a place sacred to the Iroquois people for its healing spring at the High Rock. They called it "The Medicine Spring of the Great Spirit." If it is true that all of our stories come first from the earth then I have been blessed with good earth to listen to.

II. The People of the Longhouse

No Native American people was more important in the shaping of U.S. history than the Iroquois. Their great confederacy of Five Nations, the Mohawk, the Oneida, the Onondaga, the Cayuga and the Seneca (joined later by the dispossessed Tuscarora) was the creation of two great teachers. Those men, Hiawatha and The Peacemaker were supported in their efforts by the most powerful of all Iroquois women, Jigonsaseh. The story of how they brought together the formerly warring nations of the Longhouse is a true American epic.

Not only was the Iroquois League a strong military power, one courted by the various European nations and the force which surely swung the balance to England in the French and Indian Wars, it was also a model of diplomacy and co-existence and it welcomed many non-Iroquois peoples to "come under the Great Tree of Peace." At the height of their power, the Iroquois controlled that part of the continent which was then most crucial for trade and travel, an area which included most of present-day New York, Pennsylvania and Ohio. There is good evidence that the form of the Iroquois League was the model for the structure of the United States Constitution.

The main dwelling of the Iroquois people was the elm bark longhouse, a more or less rectangular structure with an eastward-facing entrance door, a central fire and compartments to either side, one for each family. Some of the old longhouses were more than 200 feet long and 50 feet wide. The women were the heads of the families and, though the men spoke in council, it was the women who decided which men would be chosen to speak. Clan was inherited through the mother and each longhouse was headed by a clan mother. The clans found among the Iroquois nations included the Bear, the Wolf, the Turtle, the Snipe, the Hawk, the Deer, the Heron and the Beaver.

The Iroquois people lost most of their ancestral lands and political power following the Revolutionary War through unfair treaties and blatantly dishonest land deals. Though their current land base is limited to approximately seventeen small reservations and communities in the United States and Canada, there are more than 50,000 Iroquois people today and they are increasingly conscious of their significant past and the role they can continue to play. Their ideals of peace for all human beings and balance with the natural world are lessons which Iroquois people say all of us still need to learn.

III. The Storytellers

Wherever I've visited Native American people, I've heard stories. Sometimes they've been told in traditional settings—in a sweat lodge or around a fire—other times at a kitchen table while kids in the next room watched reruns of M*A*S*H. The strength of the traditional tales has not diminished, though the settings of Native American life may change. The stories last because of their continuing role in American Indian life. They entertain, they instruct, and they empower. Although told first for Native American people, they also may be of use to any human being who wishes to live in a good relationship with the world and the beings around us.

Among the Iroquois, the storyteller was often an older relative, perhaps a grandparent, an aunt or uncle, someone who remembered the stories from long ago. Although young people learned stories at an early age, it was almost always one of the older men or women who did the actual telling, since elders were always treated with great deference. Modesty was important, however, and it was not unusual for a storyteller to begin: "I cannot tell these tales as they used to be told."

There were also those who were more or less "professional" storytellers. Since they travelled about from place to place, these storytellers were usually men of vigorous health in late middle age. Among the Seneca nation of the Iroquois, such a storyteller was known as *Hageota*, "one who stories." Those storytellers often would carry a storytelling pouch, filled with such things as animal claws, various feathers, a corn husk doll, a flint arrowhead—items which would remind the storyteller of a particular legend when he pulled something out at random. Good luck was said to follow a good storyteller and he was welcomed wherever he travelled. After the stories, those who had gathered to take part in the experience would each give the storyteller a small present, perhaps a bundle of tobacco or some beads.

In the old days, storytellers interacted with the people. Every now and then the storyteller might ask a question—expecting an answer from the participant audience—or say a word such as this: "Ho?" And those who were still awake and listening would answer "Henh!"

Ho?

Further Reading

Tales of the Iroquois, Volumes I and II by Tehenetorens, Akwesasne Notes Press. Volume I contains Iroquois picture writing and versions of a number of traditional stories. Volume II contains historical accounts of the migration of the Iroquois, the Formation of the League and the Code of the prophet Handsome Lake.

Iroquois Arts, A Directory of a People and Their Work, edited by Christina B. Johannsen and John P. Ferguson, Association for the Advancement of Native North American Arts and Crafts, 1983. This 406 page, 9" x 12" volume contains, with many photographs of both artists and their work, information about hundreds of contemporary Iroquois people and the artwork they create, from baskets to stonecarving.

5

League of the Iroquois by Lewis Henry Morgan. Published in 1851, this remains the classic description of the Iroquois people and their league. Morgan's main source of information, Ely Parker, was himself one of the most interesting men of his time. Great-uncle to Arthur Parker, Ely Parker's Indian name was Donehogawa and he was both a Grand Sachem of the Seneca and a General in the Union Army during the Civil War.

Parker On The Iroquois, edited by William Fenton, Syracuse University Press, 1968. Contains significant essays by Arthur Parker on The Constitution of the Six Nations, Iroquois uses of Maize and other food plants, and the Code of Handsome Lake.

Akwesasne Notes, a newspaper edited by the Mohawk people and published from the Mohawk Nation in northern New York State. Now in its 16th year, *Akwesasne Notes* contains articles, art work, poetry and cartoons. Sometimes controversial, it is always informative and lively. A subscription costs $8 and can be ordered from *Akwesasne Notes*, Mohawk Nation via Rooseveltown, NY 13683.

'I will now tell a story.''

I Will Now tell a Story

It is the time of deep snow. Within the longhouse, people have settled into the rhythms of winter. At times, the wind blows down through the hole in the roof above the central fire and fills the air with smoke so thick that families on one side of the great building can barely see people thirty feet away on the other side.

People sit on robes of animal skin and busy themselves with the repair of clothing and weapons. They carve stone pipes and decorate ceremonial costumes with quill work. When the weather is cold and clear, the men walk out to play the snowsnake game. They drag a log across the snow to make a groove. Then they fling long sticks along the track as far as they can go, betting on whose "snake" will go farthest. Sometimes the best player can throw his snowsnake so that it whistles along the packed crust for almost a mile.

In the old days, the long months between first frost and spring thaw were not spent merely waiting for the warm breath of spring. On the contrary, it was a time many people looked forward to eagerly, especially the children, for it was a time when the storytellers would once again tell the tales of wonder.

Imagine the fire at the center of an elm bark longhouse. Imagine people of all ages gathered around the old man or woman who knows how things came to be and why things are as they are, the stories which teach human beings to live in balance.

It is many years ago . . . and it is now. The old longhouses are all gone, their walls of elm bark fallen away into the earth. But the people of the longhouse, the Iroquois, still live and the snowsnake game is still played. And in the new longhouses, white wooden buildings which resemble old country schoolhouses, traditional Iroquois still gather around the wood stove to listen to the old stories. While some of the Iroquois still remember the gifts of life given them by their Grandmother, the Earth, and their creator, the Good Mind, others will watch the television set flicker the myths of another people, myths which are pale in comparison to the old tales.

The buffalo are gone from the salt licks near Onondaga Lake and the Iroquois people drive cars to work in the morning. But as a wise leader of the Senecas said, "Our religion is not a thing of paint and feathers, but of the heart." So it is true of the stories of the Hotinonsonni, the longhouse people. These stories do not need longhouses, or central fires, or fur robes, or ceremonial garments to come alive.

*   *   *

9

Now the old person raises a hand. Everyone is silent, waiting for the words to be spoken.

"I will now tell a story."

With one voice, the audience answers, "We are listening, *He!*"

And once again, the time of stories begins.

The boy made a present of one of the birds he had killed.

the Coming
of Legends

Long ago, in the days before people told legends, there was a boy who hunted birds. One day he had been hunting for a very long time and, because it was growing dark, he sought shelter near a great rock. As he sat there, chipping at a piece of flint to make an arrowpoint, he heard a deep voice speak.

"I shall tell a story," the voice said.

The boy was startled and looked all around him, but could find no one. "Who are you?" said the boy.

"I am Hahskwahot," answered the voice. Thus the boy realized that it was the big standing rock which had spoken.

"Then let me hear your story," said the boy.

"First," said the voice of the stone, "you must make me a present of one of the birds you have killed."

"So be it," said the boy, placing a bird on the rock. Then the deep voice told him a story full of wonder, a story of how things were in the former world. When the story was over, the boy went home.

That evening, the boy returned with another bird and, placing it on the rock, sat down to listen.

"Now," said the voice, "I shall tell you a legend. When one is ended, I may tell you another, but if you become sleepy, you must tell me so we can take a rest and you can return the following evening."

Thus it continued. Soon the boy began to bring people with him and together they listened to the legends told by the standing rock. A great many people now went to the place and listened.

Finally, the voice from the rock spoke to the boy who was no longer a boy but now a man. "You will grow old, but you will have these legends to help you in your old age. Now you have become the carrier of these stories of the former world, and you shall be welcomed and fed wherever you go."

And so it was that legends came into the world.

The two swans flew up and between their wings they caught the woman who fell from the sky.

the Creation

Before this world came to be,
there lived in the Sky-World
an ancient chief.
In the center of his land
grew a beautiful tree
which had four white roots
stretching to each
of the four directions:
North, South, East and West.
From that beautiful tree,
all good things grew.

Then it came to be
that the beautiful tree
was uprooted and through
the hole it made in the Sky-World
fell the youthful wife
of the ancient chief,
a handful of seeds,
which she grabbed from the tree
as she fell, clutched in her hand.

Far below there were only water
and water creatures
who looked up as they swam.

"Someone comes," said the duck.
"We must make room for her."

The great turtle swam up
from his place in the depths.
"There is room on my back,"
the great turtle said.

"But there must be earth
where she can stand," said the duck
and so he dove beneath the waters,
but he could not reach the bottom.

"I shall bring up earth,"
the loon then said and he dove too,
but could not reach the bottom.

"I shall try," said the beaver
and he too dove but
could not reach the bottom.

Finally the muskrat tried.
He dove as deeply as he could,
swimming until his lungs almost burst.
With one paw he touched the bottom,
and came up with a tiny speck
of earth clutched in his paw.

"Place the earth on my back,"
the great turtle said,
and as they spread
the tiny speck of earth it grew
larger and larger and larger
until it became the whole world.

Then two swans flew up
and between their wings
they caught the woman
who fell from the sky.
They brought her gently
down to the earth
where she dropped her handful
of seeds from the Sky-World.

Then it was that the first plants grew
and life on this new earth began.

Some green shoots rose from their mother's grave.

the two brothers

It was not long after
she had fallen from the Sky-World
and the earth had been made
as a place for her to stand,
that the Sky-Woman gave birth
to a beautiful daughter.
Together they lived
in peace upon this world
which rested upon the turtle's back
until the daughter became a woman.

One day she came to her mother and said,
"Mother, while I slept in the meadow, I felt
a wind sweep over me and I heard someone
whisper sweet words into my ear."

Then it was that the Sky-Woman knew
the West Wind had taken
her daughter as his wife.

Soon the daughter of the Sky-Woman
grew heavy with child
and from her stomach
the voices of two children
could be heard.

One of the voices was angry and quarrelsome.
"My brother," it said, "let us tear our way out.
I think I see light through our mother's side."

The other voice was loving and gentle.
"No, my brother," said the other voice.
"We must not do that, for it would cause
    her death."

Before long the time came
for the brothers to be born.
The good-minded brother was the first
and entered this life in the normal way.
But the brother of evil mind
tore his way through their mother's side
and she died when he was born.

The Sky-Woman was saddened
at her daughter's death.
She looked at the children
who stood before her.
"My grandsons," she said,
"your mother has gone
before us to that good place
where all who live good lives
shall dwell some day.
Let us bury her now
and something good may happen."

Then the brother
who was good of mind
helped to bury his mother's body,
while the other brother, the Evil Mind
paid no attention

and either slept or cried for food.

Soon green shoots rose
from their mother's grave.
From her fingers came the bean plants,
from her feet came the potatoes.
From her stomach came the squashes
and from her breasts, the corn.
Last of all, from her forehead,
grew the medicine plant, tobacco.

Then the Good Mind listened
to his grandmother's words
teaching him, telling him how
to shape the earth and bring good things
to be used by the humans who were to come.

When she finished, she departed,
back into the Sky-World
where she still looks down
on us through the nights
as the moon, our grandmother.

Then the Good Mind touched the earth
and from it grew the tall elm tree
which gives its bark for the lodges of the people.

But the Evil Mind struck the earth
and the briars and bushes with thorns sprang up.

Then the Good Mind touched the earth
and from it flowed the springs of pure water.

But the Evil Mind struck the earth,
kicking in dirt to muddy the springs.

Then the Good Mind touched the earth,
making the rivers and running streams
to carry people from place to place,
with currents flowing in each direction.

But the Evil Mind made rapids and falls
and twisted the streams, throwing in great rocks
so that travel would not be an easy thing.

Then the Good Mind made animals and birds
and creatures friendly to human beings,
to be his companions and provide him with food.

But the Evil Mind made evil creatures:
The Flying Heads and the monster bears,
great horned serpents, Stone Giants and beings
who would trouble the lives and dreams of the
    people.

So it was that in the two brothers
all that was good and all that was evil
came to this world and the long contest
between the Good and the Evil Minds began.

And even today, this world we walk in
is made of both good and evil things.
But if we choose the Good Mind's path,
remembering right is greater than wrong,
we will find our reward at journey's end.

"Yes, I would like to be a bear," the boy said.

the Boy Who
Lived With the Bears

There was once a boy whose father and mother had died and he was left alone in the world. The only person he had to take care of him was his uncle, but his uncle was not a kind man. The uncle thought that the boy was too much trouble and fed him only scraps from the table and dressed him in tattered clothing and moccasins with soles that were worn away. When the boy slept at night, he had to sleep outside his uncle's lodge far away from the fire. But the boy never complained because his parents had told him always to respect people older than himself.

One day the uncle decided to get rid of the boy. "Come with me," he said. "We are going hunting."

The boy was very happy. His uncle had never taken him hunting before. He followed him into the woods. First his uncle killed a rabbit. The boy picked it up to carry it for the uncle and was ready to turn back to the lodge, but his uncle shook his head. "We will go on. I am not done hunting."

They went further and the uncle killed a fat grouse. The boy was very happy, for they would have so much to eat that surely his uncle would feed him well that night and he began to turn back, but the uncle shook his head again. "No," he said, "we must go on."

Finally, they came to a place very, very far in the forest where the boy had not been before. There was a great cliff and at its base a cave led into the rock. The opening to the cave was large enough only for a small person to go into. "There are animals hiding in there," the uncle said. "You must crawl in and chase them out so that I can shoot them with my arrows."

The cave was very dark and it looked cold inside, but the boy remembered what his parents had taught him. He crawled into the cave. There were leaves and stones, but there were no animals. He reached the very end of the cave and turned back, ashamed that he had not fulfilled his uncle's expectations. And do you know what he saw? He saw his uncle rolling a great stone in front of the mouth of the cave. And then everything was dark.

The boy tried to move the stone, but it was no use. He was trapped! At first he was afraid, but then he remembered what his parents had told him. The orenda of those who are good at heart is very strong. If you do good and have faith, good things will come to you. This made the boy happy and he began to sing a song. The song was about himself, a boy who had no parents and needed friends. As he sang, his song grew louder, until he forgot he was trapped in a cave. But then he heard a scratching noise outside and stopped singing, thinking his uncle had come back to let him out of the cave.

However, as soon as he heard the first of many voices outside his cave, he knew that he was wrong. That high squeaking voice was not the voice of his uncle. "We should help this boy," said the high squeaking voice.

"Yes," said a very deep voice which sounded warm and loving. "He is all alone and needs help.

There is no doubt that we should help him."

"One of us," said another voice, "will have to adopt him."

And then many other voices, voices of all kinds which seemed to speak in many languages agreed. The strange thing was that the boy could understand all these voices, strange as they were. Then the stone began to move and light streamed into the cave, blinding the boy who had been in the darkness for a long time. He crawled out, very stiff and cold, and looked around him. He was surrounded by many animals!

"Now that we have rescued you," said a small voice from near his feet, "you must choose which of us will be your parents now." He looked down and saw that the one who was speaking was a mole.

"Yes," said a great moose standing in the trees. "You must choose one of us."

"Thank you," said the boy. "You are all so kind. But how can I choose which one of you will be my parents?"

"I know," said the mole. "Let us all tell him what we are like and what kind of lives we lead and he can decide." There was general agreement on that, and so the animals began to come up to the boy one by one.

"I'll begin," said the mole. "I live under the earth and dig my tunnels through the Earth Mother. It is very dark and cozy in my tunnels and we have plenty of worms and grubs to eat."

"That sounds very good," said the boy, "but I am afraid that I am too big to go into your tunnels, friend Mole."

"Come and live with me," said the beaver. "I live in a fine lodge in the midst of a pond. We beavers eat the best bark from the sweetest trees and we dive under the water and sleep in our lodge in the winter time."

"Your life is very interesting too," said the boy, "but I cannot eat bark, and I know that I would freeze in the cold waters of your pond."

"How about me?" said the wolf. "I run through the woods and fields and I catch all the small animals I want to eat. I live in a warm den and you would do well to come with me."

"You too are very kind," said the boy, "but all of the animals have been so kind to me I would not feel right eating them."

"You could be my child," said the deer. "Run with us through the forest and eat the twigs of the trees and the grass of the fields."

"No, friend Deer," the boy said, "you are beautiful and good, but you are so fast that I would be left far behind you."

Then an old bear-woman walked over to the boy. She looked at him a long time before she talked and when she spoke her voice was like a growling song. "You can come with us and be a bear," she said. "We bears move slowly and speak with harsh voices, but our hearts are warm. We eat the berries and the roots which grow in the forest and our fur would keep you warm in the long season of cold."

"Yes," said the boy, "I would like to be a bear. I will come with you and you will be my family." So the boy who had no family went to live with the bears. The mother bear had two other children and they became brothers to the boy. They would roll and play together and soon the boy was almost as strong as a bear.

"Be careful, though," the old bear-woman cautioned him. "Your brothers' claws are sharp and wherever they scratch you, you will grow hair just like them." They lived together a long time in the forest and the old bear-woman taught the boy many things.

One day they were all in the forest seeking berries when the bear-woman motioned them to silence. "Listen," she said. "There is a hunter." They listened and, sure enough, they heard the sounds of a man walking. The old bear-woman smiled. "We have nothing to fear from him," she said. "He is the heavy-stepper and the twigs and the leaves of the forest speak of him wherever he goes."

Another time as they walked along, the old bear-woman again motioned them to silence. "Listen," she said. "Another hunter." They listened and soon they heard the sound of singing. The old bear-woman smiled. "That one too is not dangerous. He is the flapping-mouth, the one who talks as he hunts and does not remember that everything in the forest has ears. We bears can hear singing even if it is only thought, and not spoken."

So they lived on happily until one day when the old bear-woman motioned them to silence, a frightened look in her eyes. "Listen," she said, "the one who hunts on two-legs and four-legs. This one is very dangerous to us, and we must hope he does not find us, for the four-legs who hunts with him can follow our tracks wherever we go and the man himself does not give up until he has caught whatever it is that he is hunting for."

Just then they heard the sound of a dog barking. "Run for your lives," cried the old bear-woman. "The four-legs has caught our scent."

And so they ran, the boy and the three bears. They ran across streams and up hills, but still the sound of the dog followed them. They ran through swamps and thickets, but the hunters were still close behind. They crossed ravines and forced their way through patches of thorns, but could not escape the sounds of pursuit. Finally, their hearts ready to burst from exhaustion, the old bear-woman and the boy and the two bear-brothers came to a great hollow log. "It is our last hope," said the old bear-woman. "Go inside."

They crawled into the log and waited, panting and afraid. For a time, there was no sound and then the noise of the dog sniffing at the end of their log came to their ears. The old bear-woman growled and the dog did not dare to come in after them. Then, once again, things were quiet and the boy began to hope that his family would be safe, but his hopes were quickly shattered when he smelled smoke. The resourceful hunter had piled branches at the end of the log and was going to smoke them out!

"Wait," cried the boy in a loud voice. "Do not harm my friends."

"Who is speaking?" shouted a familiar voice from outside the log. "Is there a human being inside there?" There came the sound of branches being kicked away from the mouth of the log and then the smoke stopped. The boy crawled out and looked into

29

the face of the hunter—it was his uncle!!

"My nephew!" cried the uncle with tears in his eyes. "Is it truly you? I came back to the cave where I left you, realizing that I had been a cruel and foolish man . . . but you were gone and there were only the tracks of many animals. I thought they had killed you."

And it was true. Before the uncle had reached home, he had realized that he had been a wicked person. He had turned back, resolved to treat the son of his own sister well from then on. His grief had truly been great when he had found him gone.

"It is me," said the boy. "I have been cared for by the bears. They are like my family now, Uncle. Please do not harm them."

The uncle tied his hunting dog to a tree as he nodded his agreement. "Bring out your friends. I will always be the friend of bears from now on if what you say is true."

Uncertain and still somewhat afraid, the old bear-woman and her two sons came out of the log. They talked to the boy with words which sounded to the uncle like nothing more than animals growling and told him that he must now be a human being again. "We will always be your friends," said the old bear-woman and she shuffled into the forest after her two sons. "And you will remember what it is to know the warmth of an animal's heart."

And so the boy returned to live a long and happy life with his uncle, a friend to the bears and all the animals for as long as he lived.

"Greetings, brother," said Fox. *"How are you this fine day?"*

how Bear
lost his tail

Back in the old days, Bear had a tail which was his proudest possession. It was long and black and glossy and Bear used to wave it around just so that people would look at it. Fox saw this. Fox, as everyone knows, is a trickster and likes nothing better than fooling others. So it was that he decided to play a trick on Bear.

It was the time of year when Hatho, the Spirit of Frost, had swept across the land, covering the lakes with ice and pounding on the trees with his big hammer. Fox made a hole in the ice, right near a place where Bear liked to walk. By the time Bear came by, all around Fox, in a big circle, were big trout and fat perch. Just as Bear was about to ask Fox what he was doing, Fox twitched his tail which he had sticking through that hole in the ice and pulled out a huge trout.

"Greetings, Brother," said Fox. "How are you this fine day?"

"Greetings," answered Bear, looking at the big circle of fat fish. "I am well, Brother. But what are you doing?"

"I am fishing," answered Fox. "Would you like to try?"

"Oh, yes," said Bear, as he started to lumber over to Fox's fishing hole.

But Fox stopped him. "Wait, Brother," he said. "This place will not be good. As you can see, I have already caught all the fish. Let us make you a new fishing spot where you can catch many big trout."

Bear agreed and so he followed Fox to the new place, a place where, as Fox knew very well, the lake was too shallow to catch the winter fish—which always stay in the deepest water when Hatho has covered their ponds. Bear watched as Fox made the hole in the ice, already tasting the fine fish he would soon catch. "Now," Fox said, "you must do just as I tell you. Clear your mind of all thoughts of fish. Do not even think of a song or the fish will hear you. Turn your back to the hole and place your tail inside it. Soon a fish will come and grab your tail and you can pull him out."

"But how will I know if a fish has grabbed my tail if my back is turned?" asked Bear.

"I will hide over here where the fish cannot see me," said Fox. "When a fish grabs your tail, I will shout. Then you must pull as hard as you can to catch your fish. But you must be very patient. Do not move at all until I tell you."

Bear nodded, "I will do exactly as you say." He sat down next to the hole, placed his long beautiful black tail in the icy water and turned his back.

Fox watched for a time to make sure that Bear was doing as he was told and then, very quietly, sneaked back to his own house and went to bed. The next morning he woke up and thought of Bear. "I wonder if he is still there," Fox said to himself. "I'll just go and check."

So Fox went back to the ice covered pond and what do you think he saw? He saw what looked like a little white hill in the middle of the ice. It had snowed during the night and covered Bear, who had fallen asleep while waiting for Fox to tell him to pull out his tail and catch a fish. And Bear was snoring. His snores were so loud that the ice was shaking. It was so funny that Fox rolled with laughter. But when he was through laughing, he decided the time had come to wake up poor Bear. He crept very close to Bear's ear, took a deep breath, and then shouted: "*Now, Bear!!!*"

Bear woke up with a start and pulled his long tail as hard as he could. But his tail had been caught in the ice which had frozen over during the night and as he pulled, it broke off—Whack!—just like that. Bear turned around to look at the fish he had caught and instead saw his long lovely tail caught in the ice.

"Ohhh," he moaned, "ohhh, Fox, I will get you for this." But Fox, even though he was laughing fit to kill, was still faster than Bear and he leaped aside and was gone.

So it is that even to this day Bears have short tails and no love at all for Fox. And if you ever hear a Bear moaning, it is probably because he remembers the trick Fox played on him long ago and he is mourning for his lost tail.

"Oh, Bear," Chipmunk said, "you are right to kill me, I deserve to die. Just please let me say one word to Creator before you eat me."

Chipmunk
and Bear

Long ago when animals could talk, a bear was walking along. Now it has always been said that bears think very highly of themselves. Since they are big and strong, they are certain that they are the most important of the animals.

As this bear went along turning over big logs with his paws to look for food to eat, he felt very sure of himself. "There is nothing I cannot do," said this bear.

"Is that so?" said a small voice. Bear looked down. There was a little chipmunk looking up at Bear from its hole in the ground.

"Yes," Bear said, "that is true indeed." He reached out one huge paw and rolled over a big log. "Look at how easily I can do this. I am the strongest of all the animals. I can do anything. All the other animals fear me."

"Can you stop the sun from rising in the morning?" said the chipmunk.

Bear thought for a moment. "I have never tried that," he said. "Yes, I am sure I could stop the sun from rising."

37

"You are sure?" said Chipmunk.

"I am sure," said Bear. "Tomorrow morning the sun will not rise. I, Bear, have said so." Bear sat down facing the east to wait.

Behind him the sun set for the night and still he sat there. The chipmunk went into its hole and curled up in its snug little nest, chuckling about how foolish Bear was. All through the night Bear sat. Finally the first birds started their songs and the east glowed with the light which comes before the sun.

"The sun will *not* rise today," said Bear. He stared hard at the growing light. "The sun *will not* rise today."

However, the sun rose, just as it always had. Bear was very upset, but Chipmunk was delighted. He laughed and laughed. "Sun is stronger than Bear," said the chipmunk, twittering with laughter. Chipmunk was so amused that he came out of his hole and began running around in circles, singing this song:

"The sun came up,
The sun came up.
Bear is angry,
But the sun came up."

While Bear sat there looking very unhappy, Chipmunk ran around and around, singing and laughing until he was so weak that he rolled over on his back. Then, quicker than the leap of a fish from a stream, Bear shot out one big paw and pinned him to the ground.

"Perhaps I cannot stop the sun from rising," said Bear, "but *you* will never see another sunrise."

"Oh, Bear," said the chipmunk, "oh, oh, oh, you are the strongest, you are the quickest, you are the best of all of the animals. I was only joking." But Bear did not move his paw.

"Oh, Bear," Chipmunk said, "you are right to kill me, I deserve to die. Just please let me say one last prayer to Creator before you eat me."

"Say your prayer quickly," said Bear. "Your time to walk the Sky Road has come!"

"Oh, Bear," said Chipmunk, "I would like to die. But you are pressing down on me so hard I cannot breathe. I can hardly squeak. I do not have enough breath to say a prayer. If you would just lift your paw a little, just a little bit, then I could breathe. And I could say my last prayer to the Maker of all, to the one who made great, wise, powerful Bear and the foolish, weak, little Chipmunk."

Bear lifted up his paw. He lifted it just a little bit. That little bit, though, was enough. Chipmunk squirmed free and ran for his hole as quickly as the blinking of an eye. Bear swung his paw at the little chipmunk as it darted away. He was not quick enough to catch him, but the very tips of his long claws scraped along Chipmunk's back leaving three pale scars.

To this day, all chipmunks wear those scars as a reminder to them of what happens when one animal makes fun of another.

He took one step . . . and found he had become as small as the tiny hunters and was sitting with them inside their canoe.

the Gifts of
the Little people

There once was a boy whose parents had died. He lived with his uncle who did not treat him well. The uncle dressed the boy in rags and because of this the boy was called Dirty Clothes.

This boy, Dirty Clothes, was a good hunter. He would spend many hours in the forest hunting food for his lazy uncle who would not hunt for himself.

One day Dirty Clothes walked near the river, two squirrels that he had shot hanging from his belt. He walked near the cliffs which rose from the water. This is where the Little People, the Jo-Ge-Oh, often beat their drums. Most of the hunters from the village were afraid to go near this place, but Dirty Clothes remembered the words his mother had spoken years ago, "Whenever you walk with good in your heart, you should never be afraid."

A hickory tree grew there near the river. He saw something moving in its branches. A black squirrel was hopping about high up in the top of the tree. Then Dirty Clothes heard a small voice. "Shoot again, Brother," the small voice said. "You still have not hit him."

41

Dirty Clothes looked down and there near his feet were two small hunters. As he watched, one of them shot an arrow but it fell short of the black squirrel. "Ah," Dirty Clothes thought, "they will never succeed like that. I must help them." He drew his bow and with one shot brought down the squirrel.

The tiny hunters ran to the squirrel. "Whose arrow is this?" asked one of them. They looked up and saw the boy. "Eee-yah," said one of the tiny hunters, "you have shot well. The squirrel is yours."

"Thank you," Dirty Clothes answered, "but the squirrel is yours and also these others I have shot today."

The two small hunters were very glad. "Come with us," they said. "Come visit our lodge so we can thank you properly."

Dirty Clothes thought about his uncle, but it was still early in the day and he could hunt some more after visiting them. "I will come with you," Dirty Clothes said.

The two Little People led the boy to the river. There a tiny canoe was waiting, only as big as one of his shoes, but his friends told him to step inside. He took one step . . . and found he had become as small as the tiny hunters and was sitting with them inside their canoe.

The Little People dipped their paddles and up the canoe rose into the air! It flew above the hickory tree, straight to the cliffs and into a cave, the place where the Jo-Ge-Oh people lived. There the two hunters told their story to the other Little People gathered there who greeted the boy as a friend. "You must stay with us," his new friends said, "for just a short time so we can teach you."

Then the Jo-Ge-Oh taught Dirty Clothes things which he had never known. They told him many useful things about the birds and the forest animals. They taught him much about the corn and the squash and the beans which feed human life. They taught him about the strawberries which glow each June like embers in the grass and showed him how to make a special drink which the Little People love.

Last they showed him a new dance to teach his people, a dance to be done in a darkened place so the Little People could come and dance with them unseen, a dance which would honor the Jo-Ge-Oh and thank them for their gifts.

Four days passed and the boy knew that the time had come for him to leave. "I must go to my village," he told his friends.

So it was that with the two small hunters he set out walking towards his home. As they walked with him, his two friends pointed to the many plants which were useful and the boy looked at each plant carefully, remembering its name. Later, when he turned to look back at his friends, he found himself standing all alone in a field near the edge of his village.

Dirty Clothes walked into his village wondering how so many things had changed in just four days. It was the same place, yet nothing was the same. People watched him as he walked and finally a woman came up to him. "You are welcome here, Stranger," said the woman. "Please tell us who you are."

"Don't you know?" he answered. "I am Dirty Clothes."

"How can that be?" said the woman. "Your clothing is so beautiful."

At that, he saw his old rags were gone. The clothing he wore now was of fine new buckskin, embroidered with moose hair and porcupine quills.

"Where is my uncle," he asked the woman, "the one who lived there in that lodge and had a nephew dressed in rags?"

Then an old man spoke up from the crowd. "Ah," said the old man, "that lazy person? He's been dead many years and why would a fine young warrior like you look for such a man?"

Dirty Clothes looked at himself and saw he was no longer a boy. He had become a full-grown man and towered over the people of his village. "I see," he said, "the Little People have given me more gifts than I thought." And he began to tell his story.

The wisest of the old men and women listened well to this young warrior. They learned many things by so listening. That night all his people did the Dark Dance to thank the Jo-Ge-Oh for their gifts and, in the darkness of the lodge, they heard the voices of the Little People joining in the song, glad to know that the human beings were grateful for their gifts.

And so it is, even to this day, that the Little People remain the friends of the people of the longhouse and the Dark Dance is done, even to this day.

three tales about turtle

Although you would not think it to look at him, Turtle is one of the most clever of the animals and has a very high opinion of himself. Perhaps this is because he knows that the world tree, whose branches shelter us all, grows from the back of a Great Turtle. Here are three stories about Turtle, two in which he used his cleverness to beat an enemy, and one in which he allowed his own good opinion of himself to overcome his common sense.

Beaver swung his tail over his head, throwing Turtle
through the air like a bird.

turtle's Race
with Beaver

Turtle lived in a quiet pool in the big Swamp. There were plenty of fish for him to catch and trees lined the edges of his fishing hole. One day the sun was very hot and Turtle grew sleepy. He crawled onto the mud bank at the edge of his pool, made himself comfortable and soon was fast asleep. He must have slept much longer than he intended, for when he woke up something was definitely wrong. There was water all around him and even over his head! He had to swim and swim to reach the surface and, as he poked his head up into the air, he heard a loud, earsplitting WHAP!

Turtle looked around and soon saw another animal swimming toward him. The animal had big front teeth and a large wide tail. "What are you doing in my pond?" Turtle called out to the animal.

"Your pond? This is my pond and I am Beaver! I built that dam over there and made this place."

Turtle looked. It was true, there was a big dam across the stream, and it had been made from many of Turtle's favorite trees which Beaver had cut down with his sharp teeth. Other trees, which Beaver had cut to eat their sweet bark, were lying on their sides all around the pond.

"No," Turtle said, "this was my private fishing pond before you came with your dam. I will break your dam and drive you away."

Beaver whistled loudly and slapped the water with his big tail so loudly that Turtle jumped. "Go ahead," Beaver said, "but if you break down my dam, my brothers and my cousins will come back and build it again, and they will gnaw your head off too!"

Turtle began to think. It was obvious that he could not drive Beaver away by force. He would have to use his wits. "I propose we have a contest," Turtle said. "The winner will stay and the loser will go away forever."

"Good," said Beaver. "Let us see who can stay under the water the longest. I will surely win, for I can stay under the water for a year."

Turtle was not pleased to hear that, for he had been planning to propose the same contest and it was obvious now that Beaver could beat him. "No," said Turtle, "that would be too easy a contest for me to win. I have a better idea. We will have a swimming race."

Beaver agreed to that and allowed Turtle to set the course. "We will start from this stump," Turtle said, "and see who can get to the other side of the pond the fastest. In order to make it fair, since I am such a good swimmer, I will start from behind you."

The two of them made ready, and at Turtle's signal

began swimming as fast as they could. Beaver was faster than Turtle, but before he could completely outdistance his rival, Turtle stuck out his long neck and grabbed Beaver by the tail with his jaws. This made Beaver very angry, and he swam as fast as he could, hoping to make Turtle let go. When Turtle grabs something with his jaws, though, he does not let go until he is ready and Beaver could not shake him loose.

Finally, determined to shake loose his enemy, Beaver swung his tail over his head, throwing Turtle through the air like a bird. This was just what Turtle had hoped for; he landed far ahead of Beaver and easily reached the finish line first.

Thus Beaver lost the great race with Turtle and had to desert his dam, while Turtle, the crafty one, won back his private fishing hole.

Now Bear began to run in earnest.

turtle's Race
with Bear

It was an early winter, cold enough so that the ice
had frozen on all the ponds and Bear, who had not
yet learned in those days that it was wiser to sleep
through the White Season, grumbled as he walked
through the woods. Perhaps he was remembering a
trick another animal had played on him, perhaps he
was just not in a good mood. It happened that he
came to the edge of a great pond and saw Turtle
there with his head sticking out of the ice.

"Hah," shouted Bear, not even giving his old
friend a greeting. "What are you looking at, Slow
One?"

Turtle looked at Bear. "Why do you call me slow?"

Bear snorted. "You are the slowest of the animals.
If I were to race you, I would leave you far behind."
Perhaps Bear never heard of Turtle's big race with
Beaver and perhaps Bear did not remember that Tur-
tle, like Coyote, is an animal whose greatest speed is
in his wits.

"My friend," Turtle said, "let us have a race to see
who is the swiftest."

51

"All right," said Bear. "Where will we race?"

"We will race here at this pond and the race will be tomorrow morning when the sun is the width of one hand above the horizon. You will run along the banks of the pond and I will swim in the water."

"How can that be?" Bear said. "There is ice all over the pond."

"We will do it this way," said Turtle. "I will make holes in the ice along the side of the pond and swim under the water to each hole and stick my head out when I reach it."

"I agree," said Bear. "Tomorrow we will race."

When the next day came, many of the other animals had gathered to watch. They lined the banks of the great pond and watched Bear as he rolled in the snow and jumped up and down making himself ready.

Finally, just as the sun was a hand's width in the sky, Turtle's head popped out of the hole in the ice at the starting line. "Bear," he called, "I am ready."

Bear walked quickly to the starting place and as soon as the signal was given, he rushed forward, snow flying from his feet and his breath making great white clouds above his head. Turtle's head disappeared in the first hole and then in almost no time at all reappeared from the next hole, far ahead of Bear.

"Here I am, Bear," Turtle called. "Catch up to me!" And then he was gone again. Bear was astonished and ran even faster. But before he could reach the next hole, he saw Turtle's green head pop out of it.

"Here I am, Bear," Turtle called again. "Catch up to me!" Now bear began to run in earnest. His sides were puffing in and out as he ran and his eyes were becoming bloodshot, but it was no use. Each time, long before he would reach each of the holes, the ugly green head of Turtle would be there ahead of him, calling out to him to catch up!

When Bear finally reached the finish line, he was barely able to crawl. Turtle was waiting there for him, surrounded by all the other animals. Bear had lost the race. He dragged himself home in disgrace, so tired that he fell asleep as soon as he reached his home. He was so tired that he slept until the warm breath of the Spring came to the woods again.

It was not long after Bear and all the other animals had left the pond that Turtle tapped on the ice with one long claw. At his signal a dozen ugly heads just like his popped up from the holes all along the edge of the pond. It was Turtle's cousins and brothers, all of whom looked just like him!

"My relatives," Turtle said, "I wish to thank you. Today we have shown Bear that it does not pay to call other people names. We have taught him a good lesson."

Turtle smiled and a dozen other turtles, all just like him, smiled back. "And we have shown the other animals," Turtle said, "that Turtles are not the slowest of the animals."

"With a war party as powerful as our own, we will soon destroy all the Human Beings in the world."

tuRtle makes
War on men

One day Turtle decided he would go on the warpath against the Human Beings. He painted his cheeks red and climbed into his canoe, singing a war song. He had not paddled far down the river before he saw a figure standing on the bank. It was Bear.

"Greetings! Thanks be given that you are strong, Little Brother," said Bear. "Where are you going?"

"I am going to make war on the Human Beings," said Turtle. "Too long have they made war on animals. Now is the time for us to strike back."

"Hah," Bear said, "perhaps you are right. I would like to go with you."

Turtle looked at the huge form of Bear and at his own small canoe. "What can you do as a warrior?" Turtle quickly asked. "Why should I take you on my war party?"

"I am very big and strong," said Bear. "I can crush an enemy in my arms."

Turtle shook his head and paddled away. "No," he said, "you would be too slow to go on the warpath with me."

After Turtle had gone a few more miles down the stream, he saw another figure waving to him from the banks of the river. He paddled his canoe closer and saw it was Wolf. "Turtle," shouted Wolf, "I hear you are going to make war on Human Beings. You must take me with you!" Turtle looked at Wolf and at Wolf's long sharp teeth. Wolf was not as big as Bear, but he was still big enough to make Turtle worry if his small canoe could hold so much weight.

"What can you do?" asked Turtle.

"I can run very fast to attack the enemy. With my long teeth I can bite them."

But Turtle was already paddling away down the river. "No," he called back over his shoulder, "you would not do to go with me on my war party. You are too fast and you would run away and leave me behind."

When Turtle had rounded the bend in the river, he saw a strange animal standing on the banks. The animal was no larger than Turtle himself and was wearing a beautiful black and white robe. Turtle pulled his canoe in to the shore.

"You," Turtle said, "do you want to go with me to make war on Human Beings?"

"That is a good idea," said the strange animal. "I know that with my secret weapon I can be of help."

"What is your secret weapon?" asked Turtle.

"I cannot tell you," said the animal, turning his back towards Turtle, "but I can show you."

The animal, whose name was Skunk, was certainly right. His secret weapon was very powerful and after Turtle had washed himself off in the river, it was agreed that Skunk would accompany Turtle.

The two of them set off down the river, only stopping when another strange animal called to them from the forest.

"Take me with you," called the animal. "I wish to make war on the Human Beings also."

"Who are you?" asked Turtle.

"I am Rattlesnake," said the long thin animal. "I have great magic in my long fangs and can kill any animal by touching them. Shall I show you?"

Turtle shook his head quickly, remembering his experience with Skunk. "No," he said, "I believe you. Come into the boat and we will go together and make war. With a war party as powerful as our own, we will soon destroy all of the Human Beings in the world!"

A few miles further on down the river was a small village of the Iroquois. It was there that Turtle decided to make his first raid. The three warriors talked over the strategy and it was decided that surprise attack would be most effective. Skunk hid himself in the bushes near the small spring where the women came each morning to fill their water pots, Snake coiled up in a pile of firewood beside one of the lodges, and Turtle pulled his head and feet into his shell after placing himself next to the overturned cooking pots.

Bright and early the next morning, a woman went to the spring to get water. As soon as she bent over to fill her pot, Skunk shot her with his weapon. This woman was very brave, however, and even though she was coughing and choking, she beat Skunk with her fists until he was almost dead and then staggered back to the village. When Skunk recovered, he crawled away into the bushes, resolving never to attack Human Beings again. Turtle's war party was now down to only two.

Rattlesnake's turn was not far off. Another woman came out for some wood to start the cooking fire. This woman had very sharp eyes and she saw the telltale coils of Rattlesnake hidden among the logs. Grabbing a handful of stones, she began to hurl them at Rattlesnake and it was all he could do to escape with his life. So many of the stones struck him, his head was flattened out and to this day all Rattlesnakes have a flattened head as a result of Turtle's war party.

Now Turtle was the only warrior left. He bided his time, waiting for a chance to strike. The chance finally came when a man walked over to the cooking pots, intending to pick one up to use for the morning meal. Instead of picking up a pot, he grabbed Turtle who shot his head out of his shell and bit the man firmly on his leg.

"Ow, Ohhh!" shouted the man, "let go of me." But Turtle would not let go. The man grabbed a big stick and began beating Turtle with it so hard that it cracked Turtle's shell in many places, but still Turtle would not let go.

"I am going to place you in the fire and burn you," panted the man, and this frightened Turtle very much.

"I have not used my wits," thought Turtle. He cried out in a loud boasting voice. "Put me in the fire. It is my home and will make me grow stronger. Only do not put me in the water."

"Ah-ha!" cried the man, "so you are afraid of the water!" He gritted his teeth from the pain and hobbled down to the river where he thrust in his leg with Turtle still holding on firmly. Turtle waited until he was deep enough and then, letting go of the man's leg, he swam away under water as fast as he could.

Ever since that day, even though Turtle still wears the red paint of war on his cheeks, he has avoided Human Beings, his cracked shell a reminder to him of what happened when he decided to make war on Human Beings.

Finally Buzzard put on a suit of clothes that was too small for him.

how Buzzard
Got his feathers

a long time ago the birds had no clothing. They spoke like people, but they were shy and hid from sight. One day they decided to hold a great council.

"We must go to Creator and ask him for clothing," said Eagle. So it was decided. But who would carry the message?

Many birds volunteered, but finally they chose Buzzard. He could fly great distances because of his long wings, and he could soar higher than any of the other birds and so come more easily to the sun-place, where Creator lived. All of the birds burned tobacco and sent their prayers up to Creator, and then Buzzard set out on his way.

It was a long journey. Buzzard flew and flew. He ate the food he had carried with him and still he was far from the place of Creator. He became hungry, so hungry that he stopped and ate some dead fish washed up on the shore below him. They were rotten and smelled bad, but his hunger was great, and he did not notice.

He continued on his way. Now he was close to the sun-place; he went higher and higher. It grew fiery hot from the sun, but still he flew up and up. The skin on top of his naked head burned red in the sun's heat, but at last he came to the place of Creator.

"I have been waiting for you," Creator said, "because I have heard the prayers of the birds. I will give you clothes made of fine feathers to take back." Then he showed Buzzard the clothing he had prepared. It was fine indeed. There were as many colors in the feathers as there are in the rainbow snake that arches across the sky after a rain, and the feathers shone so brightly that Buzzard had to turn his eyes away from them.

"Now," Creator said, "I know how hard it was for you to fly to me. You may have the first choice of all these suits of feathers. Remember, though, you may try on each suit only once."

Buzzard was very pleased. "I must choose the finest feathers," he said to himself. "Then everyone will see them and always remember it was I who brought back clothing for the birds."

He tried on a suit of bright blue and white feathers with a jaunty cap. "No," he said, taking it off, "not bright enough." And so that suit went to Blue Jay.

He tried on another suit of brilliant red and black with a tall crest. "No," he said, "I do not look good in red." And so that suit went to Cardinal.

He tried on another suit of gray and black with a scarlet vest. Again he was not satisfied, and that suit went to robin.

He put on a suit as yellow as the sun with handsome dark markings. "Too much black on this one," he said, and that suit went to Goldfinch.

Creator patiently watched Buzzard trying on one suit after another. None of them were right. Sometimes the feathers were too long. Sometimes they were not long enough. Some were too dark, others too light. None of them seemed to be just right for the messenger of all the birds.

Finally Buzzard put on a suit of clothes that was too small for him. Although all of the other clothes had grown larger or smaller to fit whatever bird chose them, this last suit of feathers was very tight. Buzzard pulled and strained. Finally he got it on. It left his legs and his neck bare; the red skin of his bald head remained uncovered. He looked at the suit. Not fine. Not fine at all. The feathers hardly had any color—just a dirty brown. They were not shiny and neat like the others. Buzzard was not pleased. "This is the worst of all," he said.

Creator smiled. "Buzzard," he said, "it is the only suit left. Now it will have to be yours."

And so to this day you can see Buzzard wearing the suit that he earned for himself. He still eats things long dead because of what he ate on his journey to the place of Creator. And though some make fun of the way he looks, Buzzard still remembers that he was the only one who could make that long journey.

Even in his suit of dirty feathers that fits him so badly, even with his head burned scarlet from the heat of the sun, he remembers that he was chosen to be the messenger for all the birds. When he circles high in the sky, he is close to Creator. Then, even in his ill-fitting suit of feathers, he is proud.

He kept on running and singing until the snow had covered the tops of the bushes.

Rabbit and the Willow Tree

Long ago, Rabbit had a long bushy tail and legs like the other animals. He was very proud of how fast he could run. He was proud of the way his tail looked when he ran. One day late in winter when only a little snow was left on the ground, when Rabbit was running through the woods he saw a willow tree. High up in the tree were some tender buds. Rabbit saw those buds and wanted to eat them, but he did not know how to climb a tree.

"Ah," Rabbit thought, "if the snow were deep, I could reach those buds." He began to run around and around the tree. Faster and faster he ran, and as he ran he sang this song.

> If only it would snow,
> If only it would snow,
> I'd run and run about,
> If only it would snow.

Perhaps Creator heard him and answered his wish. Perhaps there was magic in his words. The snow began to fall and the faster he ran, the faster it fell. He ran and ran, singing his song. Now it was growing dark, but still he ran. He kept on running and singing until the snow had covered the tops of the bushes. Still he ran around and around, singing his song.

Finally Rabbit began to feel tired. He stopped running and looked around. The snow was so deep that he could reach the very top of the willow tree. He had all the snow he wanted. He ate his fill of those tender buds and felt very pleased with himself. Now he needed a place to sleep for the night. He could not crawl under the bushes. They were buried in snow. He saw the crotch of the willow tree just above his head. He jumped up into it, made himself comfortable, and fell asleep.

Morning came, but Rabbit still slept. The sun rose higher and higher and the day became very warm. Still Rabbit slept. The snow began to melt away. Still Rabbit slept.

The Winter Spirit saw that it was time for him to return to his home in the far north. He left the land and with him went all of the snow and ice. But still Rabbit slept. Finally, late in the day, Rabbit opened his eyes. He looked around. Where was he? Then he looked down. Ey! The ground was very far below! He remembered singing for the snow as he ran, but all of the snow was gone now and he was left, high in a tree. He had never learned to climb a tree. All that he knew how to do was run, and the ground was very far below him, very far indeed!

Perhaps Rabbit would still be sitting there if he had not noticed something. When the snow went away, it uncovered the first green plants of spring. When Rabbit saw those green plants he began to feel hungry again. If only he could be down on the ground! Those green plants looked even better than the buds he had eaten the day before. Could he jump down to them? He leaned forward a little, but it made him dizzy. No, it was too far to jump. He stared again at those tender looking green plants. It made him feel so hungry that he closed his eyes, imagining how they would taste. Just then he lost his balance and began to slip out of the tree. Trying desperately not to fall, he caught his long tail in the crotch of the tree. Then, because Rabbit was so fat from eating all of the buds, his tail broke off and stayed stuck to the tree!

Down Rabbit fell, headfirst with his front paws held out in front of him. He struck the ground so hard that his front legs were pushed back. He hit so hard that his upper lip was split in half by a sharp stone sticking out of the ground.

Ever since then, all rabbits have short front legs. They no longer run like the other animals. Though they are still very fast, they leap and hop about. Ever since then all rabbits have a split upper lip— although that has not kept them from being hungry all the time. And ever since that day when Rabbit foolishly got caught in the top of the willow tree, all rabbits have had short tails. In the spring, just when the last snow is melting away, if you look at the pussy-willows, you can see the little rabbit tails which hang from their branches. They are a good reminder of what can happen when we think too much of ourselves. Sometimes, too, when you go into the woods on a winter morning after a snow, you can find the tracks where a rabbit has been running around and around, trying, perhaps, to remember that magic song which made the snow fall deeper, trying to reach his lost tail caught high in the branches of a willow tree.

That is how the story goes. Dah-neh Hoh!

67

"See if he's dead. Go and pinch him," said the Chief of the crayfish to a warrior.

Raccoon and
the Crayfish

One day Joehgah, the raccoon, was walking along. As he walked he began to feel hungry. So, when he saw a small stream, he decided to do some fishing.

"Maybe there is a fish under here," he said, feeling under a large stone with his long fingers. A crayfish was hiding there. It nipped Raccoon's finger hard with its claws.

"Eh!" Raccoon yelped, pulling his paw out from under the stone. He reached under again. This time the crayfish nipped two of his fingers! "Eh-heh!" Raccoon yipped, pulling his paw out again. He was very angry. For a moment he almost forgot how hungry he was. Then he began to think.

"You crayfish are too smart for me," he said in a loud voice. "I am about to die of hunger and I cannot catch anything to eat." He walked away from the stream into the woods. There he found some sticky pine pitch and dead leaves on the ground. He rolled in the leaves and the pitch until his fur looked very messy. He found a rotting elm log and he bit off a piece of the rotten wood and wedged it in his mouth.

69

Then he walked quietly back to the stream, rolled over on his back, closed his eyes and opened his mouth.

Some time passed and a small crayfish came out of the stream. As soon as it saw Joehgah, the raccoon, it became frightened. "It is Ongwe Ias, the man-eater!" squeaked the crayfish. It scooted back into the stream and darted back under a rock. But later, when no raccoon paws came searching for it, the crayfish became curious. Once again it crawled to the edge of the stream bank and peeked out. There lay Raccoon. His fur was dirty, his mouth was open and his eyes were closed.

"Can it be that Raccoon has died?" said the little crayfish. He crawled slowly out of the stream. Joehgah did not move. "He *is* dead," said the crayfish. He jumped back into the stream and swam as fast as he could to the place where all the other crayfish lived. "Raccoon is dead!" he shouted. "The man-eater is dead. Our enemy will hunt us no more!"

Hearing all the noise, the chief of the crayfish asked his warriors to find out what was happening. Soon they came back, bringing the little crayfish with them.

"Raccoon is dead," said the small crayfish. "His body now lies on the bank of the stream."

"How did he die?" said the chief. He found it hard to believe Raccoon was truly gone.

The small crayfish looked around. Many had gathered to listen. "I killed him," he said. "It was a terrible fight. Many times he almost had me. Finally I picked him up and threw him on the ground. Then he died."

"Hmm," said the Chief of the crayfish. "Can you take us to the place where you fought this great battle?"

"Yes," said the small crayfish, "and you will see that Raccoon is dead indeed."

So the chief of the crayfish and many others went to the place where Joehgah still lay. His eyes were closed. His feet were up in the air. His mouth was open.

"See if he is dead," said the Chief to one of his warriors. The warrior crayfish scuttled a few inches out of the water and then hurried back to safety. But Raccoon had not moved.

"Yes," said the warrior crayfish, "he is dead."

"Go and pinch him," said the Chief to another warrior. The second warrior crayfish scuttled up to Raccoon. Raccoon did not move. The crayfish reached out and grabbed Raccoon's tail hard with his claw and twisted it. But Raccoon did not move. "He is dead," said the crayfish. But the Chief did not come out of the water.

"Look into his mouth," said the Chief. Another crayfish warrior came out of the water. He crawled up to Raccoon's mouth. He crawled right inside and found the rotting wood there.

"Eh-hey!" shouted the third crayfish. "He is very dead. He has begun to rot!"

Now the Chief was convinced. He led the others out of the water. There were many of them and they formed a circle around Raccoon's body. They began to dance, singing this victory song:

Jo-eh-gah, Joe-eh-gah
No more will he trouble us.
Joe-eh-gah, Joe-eh-gah,
No more will he trouble us.

As they sang they danced closer and closer to Raccoon. When they were close enough, Raccoon jumped up. He grabbed to the left, he grabbed to the right. He caught all of the crayfish and he ate them.

Then he went down to the stream and washed his paws to clean off the pine pitch. Ever since then raccoons always wash their food when they eat. And when Raccoon was done he smiled, "Perhaps you crayfish are not too smart for me after all," and he went on his way.

"You have made yourself look like a dead tree. But I am
Ongwe Ias. I am Fox. You cannot fool me again."

Rabbit
and fox

One winter Rabbit was going along through the snow when he saw Fox. It was too late to hide, for Fox had caught Rabbit's scent.

"I am Ongwe Ias, the one who eats you!" barked Fox. "You cannot escape me!"

Rabbit began to run for his life. He ran as fast as he could around trees and between rocks, making a great circle in the hope that he would lose Fox. But when he looked back he saw that Fox was gaining on him. "I am Ongwe Ias," Fox barked again. "You cannot escape."

Rabbit knew that he had to use his wits. He slipped off his moccasins and said, "Run on ahead of me." The moccasins began to run, leaving tracks in the snow. Then, using his magic power, Rabbit made himself look like a dead, half-rotten rabbit and lay down by the trail.

When Fox came to the dead rabbit, he did not even stop to sniff at it. "This meat has gone bad," he said.

Then, seeing the tracks that led on through the snow, he took up the chase again and finally caught up with Rabbit's old moccasins.

"Hah," Fox snarled, "this time he has fooled me. Next time I will eat the meat no matter how rotten it looks." He began to backtrack. Just as he expected, when he came to the place where the dead rabbit had been, it was gone. There were tracks leading away through the bushes, and Fox began to follow them.

He hadn't gone far when he came upon an old woman sitting by the trail. In front of her was a pot, and she was making a stew.

"Sit down, Grandson," she said. "Have some of this good stew."

Fox sat down. "Have you seen a rabbit go by?"

"Yes," said the old woman, handing him a beautifully carved wooden bowl filled with hot stew, "I saw a very skinny rabbit go by. There was no flesh on his bones, and he looked old and tough."

"I am going to eat that rabbit," said Fox.

"Indeed?" said the old woman. "You will surely do so, for the rabbit looked tired and frightened. He must have known you were close behind him. Now eat the good stew I have given you."

Fox began to eat and, as he did so, he looked at the old woman. "Why do you wear those two tall feathers on your head, old woman?" he asked.

"These feathers?" said the old woman. "I wear them to remind me of my son who is a hunter. Look behind you—here he comes now."

Fox turned to look and, as he did so, the old woman threw off her blankets and leaped high in the air. She went right over Fox's head and hit him hard with a big stick that had been hidden under the blankets.

When Fox woke up his head was sore. He looked for the stew pot, but all he could see was a hollow stump. He looked for the wooden soup bowl, but all he could find was a folded piece of bark with mud and dirty water in it. All around him were rabbit tracks. "So, he has fooled me again," Fox said. "It will be the last time." He jumped up and began to follow the tracks once more.

Before he had gone far he came to a man sitting by the trail. The man held a turtle-shell rattle in his hand and was dressed as a medicine man.

"Have you seen a rabbit go by?" asked Fox.

"Indeed," said the medicine man, "and he looked sick and weak."

"I am going to eat that rabbit," Fox said.

"Ah," said the medicine man, "that is why he looked so afraid. When a great warrior like you decides to catch someone, surely he cannot escape."

Fox was very pleased. "Yes," he said, "I am Ongwe Ias. No rabbit alive can escape me."

"But, Grandson," said the medicine man, shaking his turtle-shell rattle, "what has happened to your head? You are hurt."

"It is nothing," said the Fox. "A branch fell and struck me."

"Grandson," said the medicine man, "you must let

me treat that wound, so that it heals quickly. Rabbit cannot go far. Come here and sit down."

Fox sat down, and the medicine man came close to him. He opened up his pouch and began to sprinkle something into the wound.

Fox looked closely at the medicine man. "Why are you wearing two feathers?" he asked.

"These two feathers," the medicine man answered, "show that I have great power. I just have to shake them like this, and an eagle will fly down. Look, over there! An eagle is flying down now."

Fox looked and, as he did so, the medicine man leaped high in the air over Fox's head and struck him hard with his turtle-shell rattle.

When Fox woke up, he was alone in a small clearing. The wound on his head was full of burrs and thorns, the medicine man was gone, and all around him were rabbit tracks.

"I will not be fooled again!" Fox snarled. He gave a loud and terrible war cry. "I am Ongwe Ias," he shouted. "I am *Fox!*"

Ahead of him on the trail, Rabbit heard Fox's war cry. He was still too tired to run and so he turned himself into an old dead tree.

When Fox came to the tree he stopped. "This tree must be Rabbit," he said, and he struck at one of the small dead limbs. It broke off and fell to the ground. "No," said Fox, "I am wrong. This is indeed a tree." He ran on again, until he realized the tracks he was following were old ones. He had been going in a circle. "That tree!" he said.

He hurried back to the place where the tree had been. It was gone, but there were a few drops of blood on the ground where the small limb had fallen. Though Fox didn't know it, the branch he had struck had been the end of Rabbit's nose, and ever since then rabbits' noses have been quite short.

Leading away into the bushes were fresh rabbit tracks. "Now I shall catch you!" Fox shouted.

Rabbit was worn out. He had used all his tricks, and still Fox was after him. He came to a dead tree by the side of the trail. He ran around it four times and then, with one last great leap, jumped into the middle of some blackberry bushes close by. Then, holding his breath, he waited.

Fox came to the dead tree and looked at the rabbit tracks all around it. "Hah," Fox laughed, "you are trying to trick me again." He bit at the dead tree, and a piece of rotten wood came away in his mouth. "Hah," Fox said, "you have even made yourself taste like a dead tree. But I am Ongwe Ias, I am Fox. You cannot fool me again."

Then, coughing and choking, Fox ate the whole tree. From his hiding place in the blackberry bushes, Rabbit watched and tried not to laugh. When Fox had finished his meal he went away, still coughing and choking and not feeling well at all.

After a time, Rabbit came out of his hiding place and went on his way.

Fox closed his eyes and opened his mouth so that his tongue hung out in the dirt. Not moving a muscle, he waited.

the hungry fox and the Boastful Suitor

One day Fox was out walking along. He'd been hunting but had no luck. It was a long time since he'd eaten. His stomach was growling so loudly he could hardly hear anything else. Suddenly he realized someone was coming singing a song. Quicker than the flick of a wren's tail Fox leaped off the path and crouched down on his belly in the bushes. Louder and louder grew the song. Then Fox saw something begin to appear over the crest of the hill. It was a single heron feather. Fox moved his front paws, getting ready to leap out at the bird he thought the feather was attached to. But as the feather lifted higher and higher, he realized it was no bird at all. It was the feather attached to the top of a gustoweh, the head-dress of an Iroquois man whose face now bobbed into sight as he came over the hill on horseback.

If he sees me, Fox thought, *I can forget about my hunger forever!* It was well-known that fox skins were prized by the Iroquois. Fox tried to make himself smaller than a mouse, hoping he wouldn't be seen.

Closer and closer the man came. He was wearing

fine clothes and Fox could hear the words of the man's song very clearly now. It was a boasting song.

"No one is braver than Heron Feather," sang the young man.

"And I should know that for I am he.

No one wears finer clothing.

No one is a better fisherman.

If you doubt this, look and see."

He was on his way to the lodge of a young woman he had been watching for some time. He was going to try to impress her and her mother so that the girl would ask him to marry her. His song and his fine clothing were part of the plan.

But Fox was no longer listening to Heron Feather's song. He was not seeing those fine clothes. All of Fox's attention was on what he was smelling. Fish! That large bag hanging from the young man's blanketroll was full of fish! Fox's mouth watered and his tongue hung out. It had been such a long time since he had eaten fish. His fears left him. The young man on the horse passed him by, but Fox's thoughts were far ahead.

Yes, Fox said to himself. *I think there is a way.* As quickly as he could, he ran along through the woods, keeping out of sight of the road. Soon he was ahead of the Iroquois man. Just around a bend, Fox laid himself down by the edge of the path. He closed his eyes and opened his mouth so that his tongue hung out in the dirt. Not moving a muscle, he waited. Soon he began to hear Heron Feather's boasting song.

Heron Feather was so intent on his singing, trying to find a few more words to describe just how fine he looked in his new white buckskin breechclout that he almost rode right past Fox. When he saw Fox out of the corner of his eye, he stopped. "Enh," he said, "what is this?" He climbed down from his horse.

"Kweh, a dead fox?" Picking up a long stick he carefully prodded the side of the animal. It did not move. "Nyoh," he said, "it is surely dead." He bent down and looked at it closely. It was skinny, but the pelt was in fine condition. He picked it up by the tail. "Hmm, it has not been dead for long. It only stinks a little bit." When he said that, Fox's mouth opened a little and his lips curled back from his teeth, but Heron Feather did not notice.

"Hmm," Heron Feather said, "maybe I should skin it out now." When he said that one of Fox's eyes twitched a little, but Heron Feather did not notice. "Neh," he went on, "I should not skin him out now. If I do I may dirty my fine new clothes. I will just take him with me." He walked back to his horse and began to unlace the bag. "Weh-yoh," he smiled, "when Swaying Reed's mother sees this fox I caught she will know I am a great hunter. Then she will surely allow her daughter to bring me marriage bread." He dropped the fox in with his fish, laced the bag shut and climbed back on his horse. Soon he was singing again. This time it was a song about how great a hunter Heron Feather was.

Inside the bag Fox lay still for a few minutes. Then he began to gnaw at the side. When he had made a hole large enough, he began to drop the fish out, one by one. Finally, when all the fish were gone, he made the hole larger and jumped out to freedom and his best meal in many days.

Too busy with his singing, Heron Feather did not even notice. He rode all the way to the village where Swaying Reed lived. He stopped in front of her mother's lodge and sat there on his horse, singing until many people had gathered around. He sang of his beautiful clothes, of the many fish he caught (he actually had traded his mother's beaded moccasins for them), of all the animals he hunted and trapped. Swaying Reed and her mother came out of the lodge and watched as he reached back for his bag. Now he would show them what a good provider he was!

When he held up the bag and saw that it was empty with a hole in the bottom he stopped singing. Turning around, he rode silently away. He learned that day that boasting songs do not make a person great. It is one thing to find a fox and another to skin it.

"In that hollow tree," the dog said, "there is a terrible creature. We are trying to keep it within the tree so that you can escape."

the Dogs Who Saved their Master

Long ago a hunter owned four dogs. Three of them were very large and fierce. They were strong enough to hold and kill a bear. The fourth dog was small, but she was no less valuable. She was the kind of dog the Iroquois people call Gayei Nadehogo 'eda', "Four-Eyes." She had two yellow spots on her forehead which made her look as if she had an extra pair of eyes. Such dogs are supposed to have special power and indeed, though she was the smallest of the dogs, Four-Eyes led the others. She was always the first to pick up a trail.

The hunter thought his dogs very special and treated them as if they were part of his family. Each night he slept by their side. Whenever he killed any game he always fed them before taking any of the meat for himself.

It was during the Moon when the leaves change color. The hunter had roamed far from his village in search of game. For some time now the hunting had not been good. It seemed as if the animals had all been driven away and even with his fine dogs, it was hard to find a single deer. Finally, the hunter shot a fine buck. As he began to clean it, he noticed that his dogs had not gathered around as they usually did after a kill to be given their reward of the first cut of meat. Instead, all four of them stood around a great dead elm tree with its top broken off as if shattered by lightning. The hunter called his dogs.

"Four-Eyes, Long-Tooth, Quick-Foot, Bear-Killer," he said, "come."

But without leaving their places around the tree, the dogs just turned their heads to look at him. Now many hunters would have shouted at their dogs or beaten them, but this man had great respect for these animals.

"Something," he said, "must be in that tree. I must wait and watch."

So he made camp at the edge of the clearing, built a small fire, and made ready to go to sleep. However, just as he was about to fall asleep, he heard a noise from the other side of his fire. He looked up. There stood the little four-eyed dog.

"My Brother," said Four-Eyes, "you are in great danger." The hunter was greatly surprised. Never before had he heard a dog speak. He listened closely.

"In that hollow tree," the dog continued, "there is a terrible creature which has driven away or killed all the game. We are trying to keep it within the tree so that you can escape, but we cannot do so much longer. My three brothers and I will probably die, but there is a chance you can escape if you do as I say."

"Nyoh, my sister," the man said, leaning forward, "well shall I listen."

"As soon as I leave you," said Four-Eyes, "you

86

must begin to run. Take only two pairs of moccasins with you. I shall lick the bottoms of them so that you can travel as we dogs do, with the speed of the wind through the trees. Take nothing else with you. Your arrows and your club are no good against this creature. Go straight to the east from here and do not look back. If it goes well, I shall see you again."

Then the dog came around to his side of the fire and licked the bottoms of his moccasins. He put on one pair, tying the others about his waist with a strip of twisted basswood bark. As the little four-eyed dog melted back into the darkness, he leaped up, leaving everything behind him, and began to run. From the other side of the clearing he heard a terrible howl and the sound of his dogs growling as they attacked, but he did not slow down or look back.

All through the night he ran. The moon crossed the sky, casting her light on his path and then the east began to glow with light as the sun began to lift. He slowed down to rest and as he did so the little four-eyed dog stepped out from the bushes in front of him.

"My Brother," said Four-Eyes, "Bear-Killer is dead. We have held the creature for a while, but now it is on your trail. Look," she said, "there are holes in your moccasins. You must put on the other pair."

The hunter looked at his feet. His moccasins were all in tatters. He took them off and put on the other pair.

"Nyah-weh, little sister," he said, "I thank you and your brothers."

"You have thanked us many times in the past by the way you always treated us," Four-Eyes said.

"Now you must run. Head straight to the south. The creature is getting near."

Again the hunter ran. Once more he heard the awful howl of the creature and the sound of his dogs attacking. But he did not look back or slow down. All through the morning he ran and ran until the sun was high in the sky. Once more he paused for breath. The little four-eyed dog stepped out from the bushes in front of him.

"My Brother," she said, "Quick-Foot is dead. It is not going well for us. The creature is coming more quickly now, leaping from tree to tree. My brother and I will wait here and hide. We will try to pull it down. Perhaps you will be able to get away."

The man nodded. There were no words he could speak.

"One thing more," said Four-Eyes. "When you need strength, stop and drink from any pool of water by the side of the path. But before you do so be sure to step in and muddy the water. That is what you have always seen us doing and it is our secret for gaining strength from the water we drink. Now go."

The man did as she said. Once more he heard behind him the howl of the creature, this time from high in the trees. Then he heard the growling of his dogs and the sound of a large body being pulled to the ground. But he did not slow down or look back. Soon he came to a pool of water by the side of the path. He stepped in to muddy the water and drank. Then, with his strength renewed, he ran on.

Now the sun was only the width of a hand above

the western edge of the sky. The path had grown more familiar as he ran and he knew that he was close to his village. It had taken him many days to make the journey to the place where they had been hunting. But so strong had been the advice which the little four-eyed dog had given him, he made the journey back in only one day and a night. He was very tired now, though. He could hardly place one foot in front of the other and he stumbled as he made his way along the trail. His legs felt weaker than those of a newborn child. He fell to his knees.

The little four-eyed dog stepped from the bushes in front of him. She looked as tired as he and there were many wounds on her body. The hunter almost wept when he saw her. She spoke before he could say anything.

"My Brother," she said, "Long-Tooth is dead. My own time to die is coming. I shall attack the creature now. Perhaps I can hold it until you reach safety. Since it cannot come within a circle of light, maybe you will escape. If I fight well enough, the creature will be so weak that it will go away and never return.

"Do not weep for me. Only do us one last favor if you live. Come back and give our bones decent burial so the animals of the forest do not scatter them. Now run or our sacrifice will be for nothing."

The man stood up and ran. Tears filled his eyes. He summoned all of his strength and ran on into the deepening evening. Behind him he heard a terrible struggle as his small dog attacked the creature he had not yet seen, but he did not slow down or look back. On and on he ran until he heard one last yelp. Then he knew that Four-Eyes too had been killed. Now he could feel the ground shaking as if great trees were falling behind him. A howl split the night close behind him and his limbs felt as if they were filled with ice. Yet he did not stop or look back.

"Go-weh!" he called, giving the ancient distress cry of the Iroquois, "GO-WEH!!"

In the village the men who had gathered for the Feast to Honor the Dead heard the cry. Pulling down dry torches from the racks above their heads, they lit them and rushed out into the forest. The human cry was faint, but it was close to them.

Now the hunter felt the creature's hot breath on the back of his neck. "GOOO-WEHHH!!!" he called one last time and then, catching his foot on a root, he fell headlong to the earth. The next thing he knew he was being lifted to his feet by friendly hands. Above him in a circle were the faces of the men of his village holding torches of dried bark over their heads to give them light. Where were his dogs?

Then a terrible howl from the northern edge of the forest filled the air. The hunter and the others looked. There in the darkness something towered over the trees. It had long arms and its eyes were fire pits. They saw the gleam of sharp teeth from its mouth and the claws at the ends of its arms were like lance tips. Four times it screamed and then turned and shambled back into the forest.

When the next morning came, the hunter and a party of his friends went back and found huge tracks of a kind they had never seen before, leading straight to the north. There was blood on the rocks as if the creature had suffered many wounds. They did not follow the creature. Instead they continued on along the hunter's trail to search for the bodies of his faithful dogs. The first dog they found was Four-Eyes. Only her bones were left, but she still held between her teeth a great piece of flesh torn from the creature. They placed her bones in a sack and continued on. It took them two days to reach the place where Long-Tooth had died and here, too, they found only the dog's bones which they placed in the sack. Two more days passed before they reached the bones of Quick-Foot and another two before the bones of Bear-Killer were found. Yet the hunter had come that far in a single night and a day.

The hunter brought the bones of his four dogs back to his village and buried them beneath the floor of his lodge.

From that time on, the hunting was good for that man and the people of his village. The terrible creature was never seen again. It is said, too, that in that village the dogs were always treated well and whenever a dog was born with two spots over its eyes, it was treated the best of all.

The Chief of the village shouted, "We surrender to you. We have done you a great wrong. Have mercy on us."

Battle With
the Snakes

There was a man who was not kind to animals. One day when he was hunting, he found a rattlesnake and decided to torture it. He held its head to the ground and pierced it with a piece of bark. Then, as it was caught there, he tormented it.

"We shall fight," he said and then burned the snake until it was dead. He thought this was a great jest and so, whenever he found a snake, he would do the same thing.

One day another man from his village was walking through the forest when he heard a strange sound. It was louder than the wind hissing through the tops of tall pine trees. He crept closer to see. There, in a great clearing, were many snakes. They were gathered for a war council and as he listened in fright he heard them say:

"We shall now fight with them. Djisdaah has challenged us and we shall go to war. In four days we shall go to their village and fight them."

The man crept away and then ran as fast as he could to his village to tell what he had heard and seen. The chief sent other men to see if the report was true. They returned in great fright.

"Ahhhh," they said, "it is so. The snakes are all gathering to have a war."

The chief of the village could see that he had no choice. "We must fight," he said and ordered the people of the village to make preparations for the battle. They cut mountains of wood and stacked it in long piles all around the village. They built rows of stakes close together to keep the snakes out. When the fourth day came, the chief ordered that the piles of wood be set on fire. Just as he did so they heard a great noise, like a great wind in the trees. It was the noise of the snakes, hissing as they came to the village to do battle.

Usually a snake will not go near a fire, but these snakes were determined to have their revenge. They went straight into the flames. Many of them died, but the living snakes crawled over the bodies of the dead ones and continued to move forward until they reached the second row of stakes.

Once again, the chief ordered that the piles of wood in the second row of defense be set on fire. But the snakes crawled straight into the flames, hissing their war songs, and the living crawled over the bodies of the dead. It was a terrible sight. They reached the second row of stakes and, even though the people fought bravely, it was no use. The snakes were more numerous than fallen leaves and they could not be stopped. Soon they forced their way past the last row of stakes and the people of the village were fighting for their lives. The first man to be killed was Djisdaah, the one who had challenged the snakes to battle.

It was now clear they they could never win this battle. The chief of the village shouted to the snakes who had reached the edge of the village: "Hear me, my brothers. We surrender to you. We have done you a great wrong. Have mercy on us."

The snakes stopped where they were and there was a great silence. The exhausted warriors looked at the great army of snakes and the snakes stared back at them. Then the earth trembled and cracked in front of the human beings. A great snake, a snake taller than the biggest pine tree, whose head was larger than a great longhouse, lifted himself out of the hole in the earth.

"Hear me," he said. "I am the chief of all the snakes. We shall go and leave you in peace if you will agree to two things."

The chief looked at the great snake and nodded his head. "We will agree, Great Chief," he said.

"It is well," said the Chief of the Snakes. "These are the two things. First, you must always treat my people with respect. Secondly, as long as the world stands, you will never name another man Djisdaah."

And so it was agreed and so it is, even today.

As the boy fed the beetle grubs to the snake, its four eyes grew brighter and it coiled around his wrist.

the
two-headed snake

Once a village of the Seneca people stood on a hill above the shores of Canandaigua Lake. Their town was a beautiful one with many lodges. A tall wooden stockade built around the whole town protected them from any enemies who might attack. But, unless there was trouble, the gate stood open to welcome any who came there.

One day, in the Moon When the People Give Thanks for the Green Corn, a boy named Hahjanoh was out hunting for squirrels with his bow and arrows. He thought he heard something near his feet and looking down he saw a very wonderful thing. It was a snake with two heads. One of the heads was blue and the other was red, while its body was pale as snow. It lay there so limply that the boy knew it was not well.

"Enh?" said Hahjanoh, "little one, are you hungry?"

The snake lifted one of its heads weakly as if in answer to his question. Hahjanoh searched until he found some beetle grubs in a rotting log. As he fed them to the snake, its four eyes grew brighter and it coiled around his wrist. It was the most beautiful creature Hahjanoh had ever seen.

"Well, little one," Hahjanoh said, "there can be no harm in taking you home with me." And so he did.

Everyone thought the snake with two heads was a beautiful thing. They stroked it and praised Hahjanoh for his kindness in caring for a starving creature. All through the long season of snows he kept the snake in his home and fed it every day, pleased at the way it grew under his care. Soon it was large enough to eat first small birds and then squirrels. Before too many seasons had come and gone Hahjanoh found himself hunting all the time for the snake which now ate anything he could find. But the boy did not mind. He thought of it as his friend and was pleased at how it had grown.

Now the two-headed snake was so large that when it reared up its heads it was taller than a man. People came to see it while Hahjanoh was out hunting, marvelling at its beauty. One day, though, two children came to look at the snake. As it lifted its heads and stared into their eyes, a strange thing happened. They began to walk closer and closer to the snake as it swayed back and forth. Then the bigger of the two boys pushed the other one in front of him. He stood watching as the great snake wrapped itself around the smaller boy and then swallowed him whole.

When Hahjanoh returned that evening, bearing the carcass of a small deer to share with his friend, he found the snake gone. A trail of crushed grass led into the woods as if it had crawled away, but the two-headed snake was not to be seen.

"My friend," Hahjanoh called, "come and eat,"

but the snake did not come.

As the days went on, the two-headed snake did not return. Things began to be very strange in the village. Each day, children were missing. Some thought they had been kidnapped by enemies, yet there had been no sign of a war party. Other children in the village were acting strangely also. Their eyes were cast down, and they seemed as if asleep when they walked about.

One night Hahjanoh had a dream. In the dream his spirit protector, a great water bird, flew down. "Beware the eyes of false friends," said the spirit protector. Then it was gone.

The next morning Hahjanoh woke before dawn. He went out of the village and hid behind a large stone. Soon he saw a strange sight. From the village came the children who had been acting strangely. With them were other children whom they led by the hand. They passed the rock where Hahjanoh was hiding and went into the woods. Keeping far enough behind so he would not be seen, Hahjanoh followed.

Before too long they came to a place where there was a crevice between the rocks. Down into the crevice went the children. Hahjanoh followed. There, at the bottom of the crevice was his friend, the beautiful two-headed snake. Now it was so large that its body was bigger around than a tall pine tree. The two heads lifted above the children who came closer to it. The blue head and the red head swayed together in a hypnotic rhythm and the children swayed with it. The eyes of the snake glowed with hunger and Hahjanoh, remembering the words of his spirit protector, looked away. When he looked back again he saw that the children who had been led towards the great snake were gone.

With tears in his eyes Hahjanoh ran back to the village. How could it be that one whom they fed and saved from starving could treat his people so? He had given the beautiful snake warmth and friendship. In return it was destroying his people.

"Go-Weh!" he called as he entered the village, "close the gates. The one we treated as a brother is now our enemy."

When the children who had led the others to the two-headed one returned, they were seized by the warriors and taken to an old man who knew much of medicine and power. With a few words he cleared the mist from their eyes. They looked at the circle of faces around them like sleepers waking from a strange dream. All they could remember was having walked into the forest.

With the gates of the stockade firmly closed, the warriors waited. Since food was no longer being brought to the monster, it would now have to forage on its own. And indeed it was so. Less than a day went by before the two-headed snake came out of the woods and crawled up the hill towards the walled town. It was so long that it coiled around the whole hill. When it lifted its two shining heads they reared as high above the walls as the flight of a swallow goes over the roofs of a longhouse.

Arrows were shot. Spears were thrown. But they did not stop the great snake. The two heads lifted and fell, again and again. Many brave men were seized and eaten. Then, its hunger satisfied for a time, the snake slid back down to the base of the hill and lay there, encircling the village once more so that none of its prey might escape.

The hand of night closed over the village. Again Hahjanoh dreamed. His spirit protector flew down to him and spoke.

"String your bow," said the great water bird, "with hair from your youngest sister's head. Then wrap four strands about the shaft of an arrow. Cover the arrow's tip with a special medicine. Do as I say and you may destroy your enemy."

When Hahjanoh woke he saw next to him four feathers from the tail of a great bird. From his youngest sister's head he took strands of hair and did as his spirit protector said. He used the feathers of the bird for the end of his arrow. The tip he dipped in the special medicine. It was not yet dawn and the gates of the village were barred from within. He opened them and went out, down the hill to the place where the great snake, pale as mist, pale as a ghost, encircled their village. It was not sleeping. Four eyes, glowing as if with fire, lifted to look down at him.

"Do you know me?" Hahjanoh said. "I am the one who saved you from death, the one who fed you. I played with you and kept you warm through the long season of snows."

But the snake's eyes were cold in the faint light before dawn. They stared down into the eyes of Hahjanoh.

"Listen to me," Hahjanoh said. "How could you betray us? We treated you as a brother. Now you want to destroy us all.''

The great snake's heads lifted higher and began to sway back and forth above Hahjanoh's head. Never had their colors seemed more beautiful to Hahjanoh, but he saw the hunger in its eyes. He could wait no longer. He drew his bow and aimed at the place where the two heads joined the body.

"Wah-ah," said Hahjanoh, "so it must be," and he loosed his arrow.

Straight as a gull diving for a fish, it sprang from his bow. Other arrows had bounced off the thick hide of the great snake as if they were made of twigs, but this arrow, charmed by the medicine and the hair of his youngest sister, pierced deep into the body of the monster and cut the heart-string. Both heads jerked back in agony and the snake began to roll down the hill towards the lake. As it rolled, out of its mouth came the heads of the people it had eaten. Into the water they fell and turned into fish. At last, the great snake itself, with one last convulsion, fell into the deep waters of the lake and sank without a trace, never to be seen again.

From that day there have been many fish in the lake of Canandaigua, children and grandchildren of those who were transformed. And to this day the Seneca people tell the story of the great snake, the one who learned too late that no matter how powerful you become, you must remember to treat with gratitude those who helped you when you were weak.

The sweat lodge became red hot and burst open from the heat. The only thing remaining in the lodge was a screech owl which flew out hooting mournfully.

the Story of
Okteondon
or the
Workers of Evil

Long ago, an old man lived alone in the forest with his grandson, Okteondon. All his family had been killed by workers of evil and the old man worried greatly about the safety of the small boy. He was so worried that he hid the boy under the roots of a great elm tree which grew in front of their lodge.

One day, when the old man was out working in his corn field, he heard something. It was a song, coming from the direction of his home.

> I am rising
> I am rising
> Grandfather hear me
> I am rising

The old man dropped his basket and ran as fast as he could back to the lodge. The great elm tree had begun to tip to one side as Okteondon sang his song from beneath. With a great effort, the grandfather pushed the tree back into place.

"Grandson," he said, "you must stay where you are. Otherwise, the Eagle Women may see you and carry you away with them."

The next day the old man went again into the forest, this time gathering herbs for medicine. He had not been gone long when he heard something. It was a song, coming from the direction of his home.

> I am rising
> I am rising
> Grandfather hear me
> I am rising

The old man dropped the herbs he had picked and ran as fast as he could back to the lodge. But before he could reach it, he heard a great crash. The great elm tree had fallen. And when he reached the lodge, there was his grandson, Okteondon, sitting on the ground beside the fallen tree.

The next day Okteondon came to his grandfather. "I had a dream. I dreamt that I hunted a small bird which was black. I killed it with my bow and arrow."

"That bird," the grandfather answered, "is a chickadee. It is the first game that a boy is allowed to shoot."

Later Okteondon went out of the house with his bow and arrow. Soon he came back with a chickadee he had shot. The old man showed him how to clean the bird and cook it over a small fire. Then the grandfather sang a song.

A hunter
My grandson will be a hunter
A hunter
My grandson will be a great hunter

The old man took down his bow and arrow from the place where it hung on the wall. It was black with soot, but when he cleaned it, it looked beautiful.

In the days that followed, Okteondon had other dreams and hunted other animals, each of them right for a young hunter to shoot. First he dreamed of the raccoon, then of the turkey and finally of the deer. On the day he brought home his first bear, his grandfather grew serious; the boy had become a man very quickly.

"Okteondon," the old man said, "it is good you have become a hunter. Now our lives will be easier." He reached into his leather bag and took out a flute made of cedar wood. "This flute," he said, "will tell you what game to hunt and where to find it. Only a good hunter can use this flute, a hunter who truly respects the animals which must give up their lives so that he may live."

Okteondon took the flute and blew through it. The flute sang:

An elk, an elk
Okteondon will kill an elk.
He will go to the west
And there he will kill an elk.

Okteondon went to the west as the flute had spoken and there he found a great elk which he killed with one shot.

Each day Okteondon played the flute and each day the flute spoke and told him what game to hunt and where to find it. One day, however, his grandfather looked very worried. "What is wrong, Grandfather?" Okteondon asked.

"Okteondon," the grandfather replied, "You have become a great hunter, but I am worried about those who do evil. You must promise me not to go to the north for there is danger in that direction."

When the next day dawned, Okteondon hunted to the east. He remembered his grandfather's words but gradually his steps led him farther and farther to the left of his path until he was heading north. He proceeded in this direction until he came to a big hollow tree.

"Perhaps," he thought, "there are raccoons in that tree." He put down his bow and arrows and began to climb. He had just reached the top of the tree and was looking down into the hollow when he heard a beautiful voice.

"Come down, Okteondon, come down from the tree. Come and sit by my side and talk to me."

Again and again the voice called and, although Okteondon knew in his heart that he shouldn't listen, he kept looking at the beautiful young woman whose words these were. Okteondon climbed down slowly.

As he sat down by the young woman, she spoke these words to him gently with a smile. "Sit close to me. You look tired. Rest your head in my lap." And Okteondon did as she said, but before he fell asleep, unbeknown to her, he tied one of his long hairs to the root of the tree.

As soon as he was asleep, the young woman leaped up, put Okteondon in a skin bag, threw the bag over her shoulder and leaped into the air. She flew only a short way, however, before Okteondon's long hair, which was tied to the root of the tree, pulled her back.

Okteondon fell out of the bag and woke up. "What has happened?" he asked.

But the woman spoke to him again with gentle words and he soon fell asleep with his head in her lap. This time she untied his hair from the tree root before throwing him into her bag. Lifting the bag to her shoulder, she leaped up and flew through the air until she landed at the edge of a great cliff many miles away. There she opened her bag and Okteondon fell through the air landing on a narrow cliff.

Meanwhile, at the lodge of Okteondon's grandfather, the magic flute made of cedar fell from its place on the wall. Greatly worried, the grandfather picked it up. "Surely, something evil has happened to my grandson."

When Okteondon awoke, he saw that he was not alone. All around him were others who, like himself, had been deceived. Some had died and nothing was left of them but bones. Others were half dead. As he watched, great birds circled downward and attacked those who were still living.

A bird flew down and tore a piece of flesh from Okteondon's arm but he only laughed and spit upon the wound which healed immediately.

Meanwhile, at the lodge of Okteondon's grandfather, the mouthpiece of the magic flute was suddenly covered with blood. Fear filled the old man's heart. "Surely, my grandson has been wounded."

Okteondon lay upon the cliff for a long time, uncertain how he would ever escape. Then he had a dream in which a voice spoke to him. "Okteondon, when you wake, there will be a small cedar twig near you. Place that twig into the earth."

When he awoke, it was as he had been told. Near his arm was a cedar twig. He buried it carefully in the thin soil of the ledge. As he watched in amazement, a cedar tree began to grow and before long reached the top of the cliff. He thought he would climb the tree but knew he must do something else first.

He gathered around him all the bones of those who had died. Then he went to a big hickory tree which was growing on the ledge and began to push it. "Rise up and run," he shouted, "or this tree will surely fall on you."

All the bones came together and became living men once more. They were healthy and well except for a few whose bones had been mixed together. In one case a tall man had one leg which was too short, whereas another had an arm that was too long. (They say this is how cripples came to be.) Then Okteondon and the men climbed the giant cedar tree and escaped.

Meanwhile, Okteondon's grandfather began to despair for his grandson's life. Each night he heard a voice outside his door. "Grandfather, I am well. I have come home," but when the old man opened the door, he found only a fox or an owl which ran away quickly.

The men whom Okteondon rescued turned out to

be his brothers and cousins killed by The Workers of Evil. His kinsmen tried to convince Okteondon to stay with them, but he refused. "No, I must go and look for my wife." And he walked again to the north.

Okteondon had not gone many miles when he came upon a lodge in front of which sat the beautiful young woman and her mother.

"I have come to marry you," Okteondon said. The young woman took him aside. "You must run away from here. My mother is very evil and will surely kill you. She is the one who sent me to deceive you."

But Okteondon only laughed and returned to ask the mother if he could marry her daughter. "Yes," said the old woman, "you may marry my daughter, but you must behave in proper fashion as my son-in-law. You must promise to honor and obey me." Okteondon agreed and moved in with the old woman and his new wife.

That night as they slept, the old woman began to roll around and make loud groaning noises. "What is wrong?" Okteondon asked.

His wife answered, "You must wake my mother by striking her on the head with the corn pounder. It is the only way to wake someone who is dreaming."

Okteondon struck the old woman on the head just as his wife advised and asked, "Mother-in-law, what is wrong?"

"I dreamed," said the old woman, "that you killed the white beaver in the lake and made a feast for us."

"Is that all?" said Okteondon. "I shall do it tomorrow. Go back to sleep."

When day came, Okteondon went to the lake

where the white beaver lived. The water of the lake was so poisonous it would wash the flesh away from the bones of anyone who touched it. The white beaver rose from the water and rushed toward Okteondon, but Okteondon killed it with one arrow. He grabbed it from the lake and ran back to the lodge of his mother-in-law.

The poisonous water of the lake rose up and rushed after him, but as soon as he threw the body of the white beaver at the feet of his wife's mother the water receded. "Here is the white beaver," he said. "I have done as your dream foretold."

The old woman was very upset. "Okteondon, let me have the beaver's body." But Okteondon refused.

"Okteondon, let me have just the beaver's skin." But Okteondon refused and began to cut the beaver up in preparation for cooking it.

"Okteondon, give me one piece of the beaver's meat." But Okteondon refused. He placed all the beaver, every bit of the meat, skin and bones into a pot and cooked it.

Then he opened the door of the lodge. "You whirlwinds," he called, "You Flying Heads! I invite you to come to a feast."

Immediately the lodge was filled with Flying Heads who greedily ate every bit of the white beaver. "Hah," the whirlwinds laughed, "the old woman's brother made a good stew!" Then Okteondon's mother-in-law grew very angry and chased the whirlwinds from her lodge.

That night as they slept, the old woman began to groan and roll around again. Okteondon struck her on the head with the corn pounder. "What is wrong?" he asked.

"I have dreamed," answered his mother-in-law, "that you killed the great black eagle."

"Is that all?" Okteondon answered. "I shall do it in the morning. Go back to sleep."

The next day Okteondon set out to find the black eagle which he soon located at the top of a tall tree. He fired an arrow, but the tree grew taller and the arrow missed.

"Ah," said Okteondon, "is that how it is?" Then he took another arrow from his quiver, spoke a few words to it and fired it quickly. The arrow struck the black eagle and killed it.

Okteondon carried the black eagle back home. The old woman was very upset. Again she begged him for the body but he refused. She then asked for the skin, the meat, even one feather, but he would not agree.

He placed the whole eagle in a big pot, cooked it and invited the Flying Heads in. Soon every bit of the black eagle was eaten. "Hah!" laughed the Flying Heads, "the old woman's husband made an even better meal than her brother." Okteondon's mother-in-law grew very angry and chased the Flying Heads with such fury that several of them flew right through the side of the lodge, making great holes in the bark walls.

That night as they slept, the old woman began to groan and roll around. Okteondon struck her on the head with the corn pounder. "What is wrong?" he asked.

"I have dreamed," answered his mother-in-law, "that you went into the sweat lodge."

"Is that all?" Okteondon answered. "I will do it in the morning."

The next morning they made the sweat lodge ready. The old man built a fire and Okteondon went inside. As soon as he was inside the lodge, the old woman danced around outside the lodge and sang this song.

> Hot as flint
> Hot as flint
> Let this lodge
> Be hot as flint

When she was finished, she opened the door of the sweat lodge but Okteondon stepped out, unharmed.

"Now," said Okteondon, "it is your turn to go into the lodge." The old woman went into the sweat lodge just as Okteondon told her to. Then Okteondon danced and sang this song.

> Let it be flint
> First red hot
> Let it be flint
> Then white hot

It happened as he said. The sweat lodge became red hot flint and then white hot flint. Finally, it burst open from the heat. The only thing remaining in the lodge was a screech owl which flew out, hooting mournfully. It flapped away. The evil old woman was gone.

Okteondon and his wife went to find the lodge of his grandfather. As the old man sat before the cold fire, ashes strewn on his head as a sign of mourning, he heard a voice outside calling, "Grandfather, I am well. I have come home."

"You can't fool me," said the old man.

"Grandfather, it is Okteondon. I have returned."

"If it is truly you, thrust your hands in through the door and let me bind them to the pole."

Okteondon did as he said. When the old man realized it was indeed his grandson, he was filled with joy. He welcomed Okteondon and his new wife with great happiness and soon after, the three of them went to the village where Okteondon's relatives were now living, those whom he had restored to life.

All of them lived long and happy lives, untroubled by the Workers of Evil.

The younger sister continued hearing footsteps. At times, she could barely make out the shape of an old man in the bushes near the path.

the two
Daughters

There once was a woman who lived alone with her two daughters. Both girls were good-looking and clever and their mother was sure they would do well when the time came for them to find husbands.

When the older daughter was sixteen, the mother said, "My child, we have lived here for many years and have eaten well, thanks to our friends, the corn, the beans and the squash, but it has been a long time since we have tasted meat. You are now old enough to find a husband who is a good hunter and can take care of us. I know just the man, the son of a woman called Big Earth. They live a day's journey away from here."

"What is this man like, Mother?" asked the older daughter.

"You will like him very much. He is handsome and strong as well as being a good hunter. But now we must start making some marriage bread which you will be carrying with you on your journey."

The two girls began to work with their mother, shelling corn, pounding it and baking it into cakes of bread. It took a long time but when they were finished, they had twenty-four cakes of marriage bread which they placed in a pack basket.

"Now, my daughter," said the mother as she painted the older girl's face and combed her long black hair, "listen carefully. Do not stop to talk to anyone you meet along the way. If it grows dark before you reach the longhouse of Big Earth, do not go into anybody else's lodge. Sleep in the woods instead."

"I hear your words, Mother," said the older daughter, but her thoughts were already racing ahead to the handsome young man she hoped to marry. She lifted her basket and adjusted the carrying strap across her forehead very carefully, so as not to disturb her beautifully combed hair. Then she set out with her sister on the narrow path through the forest.

After they travelled for a time, the younger sister thought she heard footsteps following them. "What is that?" she asked.

"Oh, that is only the wind in the pine trees," said the older sister. And they continued walking.

Before long it was afternoon and the sun was beginning to bend toward the place where earth and sky meet. The younger sister listened and was certain she heard the sound of quiet feet. "What is that I hear?" she asked.

"Oh, it is only a bird," said the older sister. And they continued walking.

The younger sister, however, kept on listening. She continued hearing footsteps which were now ahead of them. At times, she could barely make out the shape of an old man in the bushes near the path.

Before long, they came to a small clearing where they saw an old man holding a bow and arrow. He

117

was looking up into a tall hickory tree. "Come here," called the old man, pointing up into the tree. "I need your help. I am trying to shoot that squirrel up there in the top of the tree, but my eyesight is weak and I am afraid I will lose my arrow."

The younger sister said, "Remember the words of our mother. We must not stop to talk with anyone along the way."

But the older sister did not listen. "This old man seems to be a very pleasant person. Let us do as he says."

"Please do," said the old man. "Put down your pack and watch my arrow. If I miss the squirrel, chase after the arrow and bring it back to me." He drew his bow and let the arrow fly. It arched high up through the top of the tree and landed many paces away in the forest. The two girls ran to get the arrow, but when they came back the old man was gone and so was the pack filled with marriage bread.

The younger sister said, "We must return home for we have disobeyed our mother."

So the girls went home and told their mother what had happened. "Ah," she said, "you must not love me very much or you would have obeyed me." She did not say anything else that night.

The next day she told the girls, "We must make marriage bread again, but this time it is you, my younger daughter, who will be the one seeking a husband." So the mother and her two daughters made more cakes of marriage bread but this time they filled the pack of the younger sister. Once more the two sisters set out on their way.

Once again the younger daughter thought she

118

heard footsteps following them but she said nothing. Instead she kept thinking of her mother's words. Late in the afternoon they came to the same clearing in the forest where the old man had tricked them. There, sitting on a log, was the old man.

"I am glad to see that you are well," he said. "Where are you going?"

The younger sister said nothing, but the older sister answered immediately, "We are going to the longhouse of a woman called Big Earth. My sister is going to ask the son of Big Earth to be her husband."

"Oh," said the old man, "you are lucky you saw me. You are going in the wrong direction. You must pass through the woods over here to reach the lodge of Big Earth."

The younger daughter was still suspicious but her sister would not listen. "This old man is trying to help us," she said. "Let us do as he says." So they went the way the old man had pointed.

As soon as they were out of sight, the old man hurried to his lodge which was at the end of the path he had shown them. "Quick," he shouted to his wife, "cover your face with ashes and sit on the other side of the fire. You must pretend to be my mother. Two girls are coming with a pack of marriage bread and I mean to have it."

The old man changed his clothes and painted his face so that he looked very young and handsome. He sat down in the shadows of his lodge. Soon he heard the sound of the two girls coming toward his door. "Enter," he called. "Come in to the longhouse of Big Earth and her handsome son."

The two girls came in and when they saw the old

119

man in his fine clothes with his face painted, they thought he was certainly the man they were seeking. They sat down beside him and put down the pack filled with marriage bread.

Just then, however, someone came to the door of the lodge and shouted. "Old man, old man, they want you at the long lodge."

"Go away!" shouted the old man and then turned to the two girls. "Someone has come to the wrong place—there is no old man here."

Before long, however, the voice returned, "Father, Father, you must come."

"Go away!" shouted the old man. He turned to the two girls. "Ah, that poor boy. His father died yesterday, and he is still wandering around the town calling for him."

It was only a short time before the voice returned again. "Please, Father, they have sent me to bring you. You must come."

The old man turned to the two girls and smiled. "I am afraid I must go and tell this child who I am. It is late and you should rest. Just lie down and I will be back soon." He went outside and the younger sister thought she heard harsh words and the sound of blows being struck.

Soon the old woman across the fire from them fell asleep. "My sister," said the younger daughter, "something is wrong. We must not stay here. This is surely the house of the old man who tricked us before. We must obey the words of our mother." She slipped out of the lodge and returned with two rotten logs. "We must wrap these logs in his blankets so that the old woman will not know we have gone."

As soon as they left the lodge, they heard the sound of dancing coming from another part of the village. Carrying the rescued pack of marriage bread, they came to a big longhouse. They looked inside and saw the old man who had tricked them, dancing in the middle of the floor while all the people watched. And there, on the other side of the fire, sat a very handsome man with his mother.

"Ahah," said the younger daughter, "that is the man we are really looking for. Covering their faces with their blankets, the two sisters slipped into the lodge and went to sit by Big Earth and her son. They placed the basket of marriage bread in front of the woman who was very pleased.

"Yes," Big Earth said to the younger sister, "you will be a fine wife for my son."

When the dancing was ended, the two sisters, still wrapped in their blankets, left with Big Earth and her son. Meanwhile the old man, very pleased with his own cleverness, went back to his lodge and saw what he thought to be the forms of the two girls covered by his blankets.

"I have returned. They asked me to come to a meeting. They can't make any decisions without me." He sat down beside his blankets and felt something pinch him. Thinking it was one of the girls, he laughed. "Be patient, I will lie down soon." Then he took off his clothes and, slipping into his blankets, found himself in bed with two rotten logs crawling with large biting ants!

The next day the two sisters returned with the son of Big Earth to the lodge of their mother. There he hunted and brought meat to the family of his new wife, the clever younger daughter who had followed the advice of her mother.

They all lived together happily.

Just then a great horned serpent crawled in through the
door of the lodge. It came up to her and stared a long time
into her eyes.

the Girl Who Was Not Satisfied With Simple things

There once was a girl who was not satisfied with simple things. Her parents despaired of ever finding her a husband she would accept. Each man who came was not good enough. "That one was too fat; he will never do." Or "Did you see how shabby his moccasins were?" Or "I didn't like the way he spoke." Such were the things she would say.

One night, as the fire flickered low, a strange young warrior came to their door. "Dah-joh," said the mother, "come inside," but the visitor stood at the edge of the light and pointed his hand at the girl.

"I have come to take you as my wife," he said. Now this young man was very handsome. His face shone in the firelight. Above his waist was a fine, wide belt of black and yellow wampum that glittered like water. On his head he wore two tall feathers and he moved with the grace of a willow tree in the wind.

But the mother was worried. "My daughter," she said, "you would not take any of the men in our village. Would you marry a stranger whose clan you don't know?"

It was no use, for at last the daughter was satisfied. She packed her belongings and walked into the night, following the handsome stranger.

The girl walked for some time through the darkness with him when she began to feel afraid. *Why had she left her mother's lodge to come with this man she had never seen?*

Just then her husband grasped her arm. "Do not fear," he said, whispering in the darkness. "We will soon come to the place of my people."

"But my husband," said the girl, "how can that be? It seems we must be close to the river."

Her husband grasped her arm again. "Follow me," he whispered "just down this hill. We have almost come to the place of my people."

The two of them walked down a steep bank and came to a lodge which had a pair of horns, like those of a giant elk, fastened above the door. "This is our home," the husband said. "Tomorrow you will meet my people."

The rest of that night the girl was afraid. She heard strange noises outside. She noticed that the lodge had a smell like that of a fish. She held her blankets tightly about her and waited, wide-eyed, for the morning.

When the next day came, the sun did not shine. The grey sky was filled with hazy light. Her husband gave her a new dress, covered just like his with wampum. "You must put this on," he said to the girl, "before you are ready to meet my people."

But the frightened girl would not touch the dress.

"It smells like fish," she said. "I will not put it on."

Her husband looked angry but he said no more. Before long, he walked to the door of the lodge. "I must go away for a time," he whispered. "Do not leave this place and do not be afraid of anything you see." And he was gone.

The girl sat there wondering about her fate. *Why had she come with this strange man?* She saw that if she had been satisfied with simple things this would not have happened. She thought of the fire in her mother's lodge. She thought of the simple, good-hearted men who had asked her to marry them. Just then a great horned serpent crawled in through the door of the lodge. As she sat there, stiff with fear, it came up to her and stared a long time into her eyes. Around its body were glittering bands of yellow and black. Then it turned and crawled out of the door.

The girl followed slowly and peered outside. All around, there were serpents, some lying on rocks, some crawling out of caves. Then she knew that her husband was not what he seemed, not a human being, but a serpent disguised in human form.

Now this girl who had been foolish was a girl who was not without courage. She knew that she would never agree to put on her husband's magical dress and become a great serpent herself. But how could she escape? She thought and thought and finally, for she had gone the whole night without sleep, she closed her eyes and slept.

Then, as she slept, it seemed to her an old man appeared in her dream. "My granddaughter," said the old man in a clear deep voice, "let me help you."

"But what can I do, Grandfather?" she asked.

"You must do as I say," the old man answered. "You must leave this place at once and run to the edge of the village. There you will see a tall steep cliff. You must climb that cliff and not turn back or your husband's people will stop you. When you have reached the top, I shall help you."

When the girl awoke, she realized she had to follow the old man's words. She looked outside the lodge and saw her husband coming, dressed again in the form of a beautiful man. She knew she had to go at once or be caught in this place forever. So, quick as a partridge flying up, she burst from the door of her husband's lodge and dashed toward the cliffs.

"Come back!" she heard her husband shout but she did not look back. The cliffs were very far away. She ran as swiftly as she could. Then she began to hear a sound, a rustling noise like the wind rushing through the reeds but she did not look back. The cliffs were closer now. Then once more she heard her husband's voice close to her whispering, whispering, "Come back, my wife, come join my people." But now she had come to the cliffs and began to climb.

She climbed and she climbed, using all of her strength, remembering the old man's promise, as her hands grew painful and tired. Ahead of her was the top of the cliff and as she reached it she felt the hand of the old man lifting her to her feet.

She looked back and saw that she had just climbed up out of the river. Behind her were many great horned serpents. Then, as she watched, the old man began to hurl bolts of lightning which struck the monsters. And she knew that the old man was Heno, the Thunderer.

The lightning flashed and the thunder drums rolled across the sky. In the river the serpents tried to escape but the bolts of Heno struck them all. Then the storm ended and the girl stood there, a gentle rain washing over her face as the Thunderer looked down on her.

"You are very brave, my child," he said. "You have helped me rid the earth of those monsters. Perhaps I may call on you again, for your deed has given you power."

Then the old man raised his hand and a single cloud drifted down to earth. He and the girl stepped into the cloud which carried them back to her village.

It is said that the girl later married a man whose heart was good. Between them they raised many fine children. It is also said that her grandfather, Heno, came back to visit her many times. Often she would fly with him to help rid the earth of evil creatures.

And when she was old, she always told her grandchildren these words: "Be satisfied with simple things."

Within the cedar box, covered with blood, the skeleton of
the wizard lay.

the Vampire Skeleton

Many years ago there was a man who was said to be an evil wizard. Though no one could prove it, it was said that in the dark of the night he would turn into an owl and go about doing bad things. When he died, no one was unhappy. He had no family and his body was placed—as was the custom in those days— in a box made of cedar wood which was left inside his lodge deep in the woods.

Many moons passed. It was the time of long nights. A woman, her husband and their small child came travelling through the woods. As they walked, the man complained. "Why is it that we must go visit your relatives? Why is it we must bring them food? We hardly have food enough for ourselves. Now we must walk through this deep snow and it is late at night."

The woman said nothing. She was embarrassed that he complained so about helping others. She trudged on ahead, breaking a trail through the snow. Their little boy rode in the cradleboard on her back. Most of the food was in the pack she carried in her arms. Then they came to a clearing. There, in front of them, was an old lodge.

"Ah," her husband said, "this is a place we can spend the night. It is a long walk to the nearest village."

The woman did not like the look of the place. "I am not tired," she said. "Let us keep walking."

But the husband would not listen. "It is decided," he said. "We shall stay here."

As they came closer to the place, the little boy woke up in his cradleboard and began to cry. It was very hard for the woman to soothe him. "If your child is not quiet," said the husband as he looked around the lodge, "I will not get much sleep." He walked over to one corner of the room where a bed had been made of spruce boughs. Near the bed was a large cedar box. "There is only one bed," said the man. "I shall sleep in it since it is closer to the door. Then if any trouble comes I can protect you and the child." He climbed onto the bed, wrapped his blankets about him and was soon asleep.

The woman made herself as comfortable as she could on the floor in the middle of the lodge. It was cold and she only had one small blanket which she wrapped around her child. Grandmother Moon's bright face was just beginning to appear from behind a cloud when she finally fell asleep.

How long she slept she did not know, but a strange sound wakened her. It was like the sound of an owl crushing the bones of a mouse. She opened her eyes slowly and looked around. Grandmother Moon's light was shining in through the open door. Her husband still lay wrapped in his blankets on the bed, but the woman sensed that something was wrong. She crept closer to look at him and saw a terrible thing. Her husband was dead. His throat had been torn out. Near his bed the cedar box was bathed in moonlight and its lid was open. She looked into it and saw an even more frightening thing! Within the box was the skeleton of a large man. The teeth of the skeleton were red with blood.

Ah, she thought, *That is the body of one who was evil when he was alive. Even death has not stopped him from thirsting for human blood. He is satisfied now, but soon he will come after me and my child. I must not let him know he has been discovered.*

Crawling silently back to the place on the floor where her baby lay wrapped in the blanket and cradleboard, she pretended to go to sleep. Then, slowly as a heron moves when it is stalking a fish, she began to move toward the open door, dragging her baby with her. When she was finally close to the doorway, swiftly as a leaping deer she sprang to her feet and rushed through the door, the cradleboard in her arms. Her feet sank in the deep snow as she ran. Now she was out of the clearing and on the trail to the village. She heard a terrible cry. "HOOO-WEHHHHH! HOOO-WEHHHH!" It was the scream of the vampire skeleton. It had discovered she was gone and was on her trail.

On she ran, on and on. Then the cry sounded again. "HOOO-WEHHHH! HOOO-WEHHHH! HOOO-WEHHHH!" It was closer than before, but she kept running. She could see that the night was ending. The light which comes before dawn was beginning to paint the eastern sky. If only she could run just a little further!

131

"HOOO-WEHHH! HOOO-WEHHH! HOOO-WEHHH! HOOO-WEHHH!" Again that awful cry came, right behind her. Her blood froze and she stumbled with fear but she kept on running. Her husband had said the village was far away, but she knew his words were only an excuse to hide his laziness. Ahead she saw a tree marked with a circle and a cross. It was the sign of a village's boundaries. She could hear feet crunching in the snow behind her as she ran but she did not look back. A clearing opened and she saw many lodges. Light flickered through the door of the closest lodge and she stumbled inside. Men and women looked up in surprise at the wild-eyed woman who stood before them holding a baby.

"A monster," she said, "outside. It chases me!" Several of the men stepped out, clutching their war clubs. There, at the edge of the village, the creature stood, its jaws covered with blood, its eyes glowing like red flames. It came no closer and as the dawn light grew stronger it turned, went back into the trees and was gone.

When the woman had finished her story, a wise old woman spoke. "I was afraid this would happen. That lodge was the home of one whose name we do not speak. He was said to be a lover of evil. Now we must go to that place and dig out the root before it grows more wicked fruits."

Before the sun was two hands high, a group of warriors came with the wise old woman and the woman who had lost her husband to the lodge deep in the woods. Inside they found the body of the woman's husband still on the bed. All of the flesh had been eaten from his body. Within the cedar box, covered with blood, the skeleton of the wizard lay. The wise old woman placed herbs inside the cedar box and in front of the doorway.

"Now," she said, "pile dry wood all around." The men did as she told them. Then she set fire to the wood. "Stand in a circle all around the lodge," she said. "Watch and see if anything comes out of the flames."

Soon the whole lodge was burning. A noise like the screaming of a man began to come from the middle of the flames. Something was running back and forth within the lodge, trying to get out. Then, just as the walls of the lodge collapsed, a huge screech owl flew out. The circle of men struck at it, but it flew into the forest.

So it was that the skeleton was destroyed. The woman who lost her husband found friends in the village. Eventually she married a man who helped her and listened to her advice. And it is said that from that time on people who died were no longer placed in cedar boxes above the ground. Instead they were buried in the earth. This way a wandering spirit would not find it so easy to escape and roam the night.

With one blow of her fist, Stone Coat Woman made a hole in the ice.

the
Stone Coat
Woman

Long ago four men went to hunt in a far part of the northern woods where they had never been before. One of the hunters brought his wife and child with him. Each day the four hunters went in different directions while the woman stayed behind to take care of the camp and her small baby.

One morning, while her husband and the others were out seeking game, the wife went to the spring for water. When she came back, she thought she heard singing coming from their elm bark lodge.

"A-uwah
So good to eat.
A-uwah
So good to eat."

The woman was very frightened for she had left her baby sleeping in the lodge. She crept closer and she could hear her baby's voice, first cooing happily and then screaming each time the song stopped.

The mother looked into the lodge. There, next to

the fire, sat a huge woman whose skin seemed to be made of stone. In her arms she rocked the small baby, singing her song. "So good to eat, so good to eat," she sang as she rocked it. Each time she stopped singing she would lean down and bite a piece of flesh from the baby's cheek. Then, as the baby screamed, she would rub the cheek with her finger, healing it completely, and begin the song once more.

The mother was terrified. She thought of running away, but she could not leave her child. Even if she did find her husband, what could he do against a being whose very skin was flint. Her only hope was to use her wits. Boldly she walked into the lodge.

"Grandmother," she said, speaking to the Stone Giant Woman, "I am glad you have come to visit us. You are welcome to stay as long as you wish."

The Stone Coat Woman looked at her and smiled a smile that was wide enough to bite the head off a moose.

"Ah, Grand-daughter," said the Stone Coat Woman, her voice rumbling like great stones rolling down a hill, "I am glad that you welcome me this way. I have come to you because my husband does not treat me well. Now that you have welcomed me as a relative, I can stay with you and help you."

She handed the baby back to its mother. Holding her child, the mother sat down across the fire from the Stone Coat Woman, waiting for her husband to come back, not at all certain what it meant to have this very special guest.

* * *

Meanwhile, in the woods to the north of the elm bark cabin, the woman's husband was having no success. Animals were very hard to find.

"Wah-ah," he said, "perhaps it is true that there are Stone Giants in these woods. It is as if something has eaten all the game."

Even as he spoke, he began hearing a sound which he thought at first to be thunder. But as the ground began to shake and the noise came closer and closer, he knew what it was. It was the sound of great stone feet pounding the earth as they walked. There was a hollow tree close by and he crawled into it, leaving his bow and arrows behind him. As he watched through a knot hole in the fallen tree, he saw two huge Stone Giants come into sight, pushing the trees aside with their shoulders as if they were reeds in a marsh.

"Ehh?" said one of the stone giants, "I thought you said you saw something good to eat, my brother."

The other stone giant looked slowly around. "It is so," he said. "I am sure it was here. Noh-KWEH! Look!" And with that exclamation of excitement, he reached down and picked up the hunter's bow— which looked like a tiny twig in his hand. "You see, there *is* good food nearby."

Within the hollow log the hunter held his breath. He prayed that the punky wood of the log would cover his scent.

"I cannot smell him, Brother," said the first stone giant, sitting down on the log which creaked beneath his weight. "Perhaps the food has moved on."

"Let us be certain," the second stone giant said, sitting down on the hollow log beside his brother. It cracked ominously beneath his weight and the hunter was sure he would soon be flatter than a leaf, but the log managed somehow to hold beneath them. "This," said the stone giant, "will tell us where the good food is." Then, as the hunter watched through the knothole, the second stone giant reached into the pouch which hung at his waist and pulled out a single finger. He placed it on his right palm and it stood upright, quivering like an arrow shot into a tree. "Pointing Finger," said the second stone giant, "show us where the good food is hiding."

With that the pointing finger bent to point at the hollow log. The stone giant reached for one end of the log, but before he could plunge his arm in the hunter ran out the other end and scooted into the trees. Putting the magic finger back into his pouch, the second stone giant gave chase and his brother followed.

The man was very swift of foot, but he knew he was no match for the long legs of his pursuers. Wherever he went, the magic finger would point out his hiding place. What could he do? Then an idea came to him. In front of him was a very tall tree with a thick branch which extended out over the trail. Quick as a red squirrel, he went up the tree, crawled out onto the branch and lay very still.

Soon the two stone giants reached the tree, but when they saw the trail ended there, they did not know what to do. Their necks were too stiff for them to look up and they were not smart enough to guess the reason why the human's trail ended so abruptly. Finally, after talking it over for some time, they remembered the magic finger. The second stone giant pulled it from his pouch. He placed it on his palm and it stood straight up, quivering like an arrow which has been shot into a tree.

"Pointing Finger," he said, "show us where our food is." But since he was holding the finger directly under the branch where the man was hiding, the finger did not move.

Now the stone giants were very confused.

"Hunh-uh," the first one said, "I knew we should have gone to hunt for moose."

"Quiet!" said the second stone giant. "I cannot think while you talk."

"Ha-a-ah," said the first one, "you cannot think while you talk either."

"What do you mean by that?" asked the second stone giant.

"Perhaps if I am quiet you will understand," said the first one.

So they quarrelled as the man watched from his hiding place. Soon the first stone giant began to beat the ground with his club. Not to be outdone, the second stone giant placed the magic finger on the ground and began to beat the earth with his club, too. They continued arguing. Realizing it was his chance, the hunter slid down the tree, grabbed the magic finger and ran.

"Little Food," the second stone giant shouted, "come back with my finger." But the hunter did not stop.

The stone giants ran after the hunter, but with the pointing finger showing him their direction the hunter was able to fool them. At last he reached a stream. Holding the magic finger high above his head, he swam across. When he reached the other side of the stream, he looked back. There were the stone giants, standing on the other bank.

"Little Quick One Good To Eat," said the second stone giant, "bring me back my finger."

"Do you mean this?" the hunter said, holding it on his palm.

"Nyoh," said the second stone giant, "bring it back over here. Then we will be very happy before we eat you."

"You are very stupid, Brother," said the first stone giant. "He will not bring it back if you tell him that we're going to eat him."

"Nyoh," said the second stone giant, "Little One Who Looks So Tasty, bring back my magic finger and I will not tell you that we are going to eat you."

"Truly," said the first stone giant, "you cannot think when you talk, Brother."

"Neh," said the hunter from the other side of the stream, "I do not want to get wet again. I will lean over and hold the finger out to you. If you lean forward you can grasp it."

"Nyoh!" said the second stone giant, "that is very good. I can use the magic finger to find you and eat you later."

The stone giant leaned over, reaching for the magic finger which the hunter held out at arm's length. He had almost reached it, when the hunter drew it back a little. The stone giant stretched further, and again the hunter drew the finger back. Three times this happened and on the fourth time, just as the stone giant was about to grasp the magic finger, the hunter snatched it quickly away. Losing his balance completely, the stone giant gave a great yell and fell into the water headfirst straight down to the bottom, and was killed. Then, leaving the first stone giant raging in anger on the other shore, the hunter stuck the magic finger into his belt and headed back to the lodge.

"My wife," he began as he entered the door, "I have such a story to tell." His words failed him when he saw Stone Coat Woman sitting on the opposite side of the fire from his wife and their little baby.

"Dah-djoh, Husband," said the wife, "our grandmother has come to visit us. Bid her welcome."

"Ee-yah," said the man, coming into the lodge slowly and then sitting down beside his wife and child without taking his eyes off the huge woman, "Grandmother, you are welcome indeed."

The Stone Coat Woman smiled. "I am glad that you welcome me," she rumbled, "for I can see you must be a strong warrior. That magic finger which you now carry belonged to the brother of my husband. If you have it, then you must have killed him. I have indeed come to the right lodge to ask for help."

Then Stone Coat Woman told her story. Her husband had been cruel to her and beaten her. Since she no longer wished to live with him, she had searched for help. If they would allow her to stay, she would help them.

One by one the other three hunters returned and, heeding the words of the hunter's clever wife, they greeted Stone Coat Woman as a relative. She was very pleased and slept that night before their door to guard them from any danger.

The next day, Stone Coat Woman asked to go with

them when they hunted. "Use the pointing finger to show the way to the game animals," she said. "I will do the rest."

So the hunter brought forth the magic finger. "Pointing Finger," he said, placing it on his right palm where it stood quivering like an arrow shot into a tree, "where can we find many beavers?" The finger pointed towards the west and the hunters went in that direction.

After a time they came to a large pond covered with ice. All over the pond were many beaver lodges. With one blow of her fist, Stone Coat Woman made a hole in the ice.

"A-uwah, A-uwah
Beavers come out,"

she sang. One by one many beavers came out of the hole in the ice and, as the beavers came out, Stone Coat Woman killed each one. The hunters skinned them, keeping the pelts and the tails and some of the meat for themselves for stew. Stone Coat Woman ate the skinned carcasses raw and was very pleased.

The next day they hunted for raccoons. Pointing Finger led them to a tall hollow tree. With one hand, Stone Coat Woman broke the tree. As it crashed down many raccoons scrambled off. Stone Coat Woman killed them all. The hunters skinned them out, keeping the pelts and some of the meat for themselves. All the rest Stone Coat Woman ate raw and was happy indeed.

Each day when they finished hunting, Stone Coat Woman would make four piles of the skins and the meat the hunters saved. The she would rub each pile with her hands until it became small enough to put into a pouch.

"Now these will be easy to carry," said Stone Coat Woman. "Only throw each pile on the ground when you reach home and they will return to normal size." And so they did.

Thus it went for many days. Each morning the hunters went with Stone Coat Woman and caught many animals. Each night she slept in front of the door of their elm bark lodge to guard them.

One morning when they woke, the hunters found Stone Coat Woman standing in front of the door. "Be silent," she said to them. "I am listening." The hunters stood in silence, waiting.

"My husband is coming," she said at last. "I hear his footsteps off to the north. He knows I am here. He intends to kill me and eat you all. If you are brave, you may be able to save your lives. You must cut four long basswood poles and sharpen them. Harden them by placing the pointed ends into the fire. Then go hide behind the great stone. When my husband comes I will fight with him. If he throws me to the ground, you must come up behind him and thrust the poles into him.

The hunter's wife put her baby into a canoe. Then she rolled up four bundles of skins to look like her husband and friends, and then paddled out into the middle of the lake to watch. The four hunters made their basswood spears and hid behind the great stone. Before long, the ground began to shake as if there were an earthquake. Smashing the trees down before him, Stone Coat Woman's husband came rushing out of the forest. He saw the figures in the canoe far out on the lake and began to wade into the water. Then Stone Coat Woman came out to meet him and they fought.

The Stone Coat Woman's husband pulled a great pine tree out of the ground to use as a club. Stone Coat Woman uprooted a great hemlock tree for the same purpose. They struck each other terrible blows with their clubs until both of the huge trees were shattered. Then they threw rocks at each other which were larger than full-grown bears. Neither one seemed able to defeat the other. Then Stone Coat Woman caught her foot on a root and fell. Immediately her husband leaped on top of her to kill her, but before he could do so, the four men ran out from behind the great stone. They thrust the basswood spears deeply into the stone giant and he died.

"Nyah-weh," said Stone Coat Woman, rising to her feet, "you have saved my life and your own. Now there are no more stone giants here to trouble you. It is time for me to go on my own way again."

Before Stone Coat Woman left, she gave a present to the hunter's wife to thank her for her hospitality. It was a piece of animal skin which had on it the hairs of many animals.

"Pull out just one hair," said Stone Coat Woman, "and your hunter will catch that animal on that day."

With the magic finger and the piece of skin, they went back to their village, taking also the pelts of many animals and much meat. There they all lived well for many years. They used their possessions to help others, always remembering they owed their good fortune to the hospitality which the first hunter's wife showed that day to a Stone Coat Woman.

She was at the base of the falls. She was resting in a big
blanket which was held firmly by three men.

the Wife of
the thunderer

Many years ago a young woman lived with her father's sister in the village of Gaugwa, close to the great falls of Neahga. Her other relatives had died of the sickness which came each year to the people of her village. Although she was beautiful, hard-working and kind to everyone, she was not treated well. She was dressed in the oldest clothing and made to do the worst tasks. Despite it all, her beauty shone through the dirt and ragged clothes. Many men thought they would be glad to marry her, but her aunt would give no man permission even to visit their lodge. As the years passed by, Ahweyoh—whose name means Water Lily—became more and more certain that she would never be allowed to marry.

Then one day, during the moon when raspberries ripen, as Ahweyoh was grinding corn her aunt came to her with a wide smile on her face.

"Make ready, Girl," the aunt said. "Tomorrow you will carry marriage bread to the man who will be your husband."

Ahweyoh's heart lifted in her chest like a hummingbird taking flight. "Who is the man I am to marry? Is it Big Tree? Is it Grey Eagle?"

"Neh," said the aunt, "I would never allow you to marry any young boaster such as those two. I have found a perfect husband for you. Tomorrow you will become the second wife of Sweaty Hands."

Sweaty Hands! Of all the men in the village there was no one more unpleasant. It was said that he beat his wife so badly that often she could not walk for a whole day's journey of the sun across the sky. His face was as ugly as his manners. He was short and fat as a woodchuck in the summer and he never had a good word for anyone. He was even said to be a coward in battle. It was rumored that the wealth he had in his lodge had been gained only by treachery or by evil medicine.

"My aunt," Ahweyoh said, "you are teasing me. Surely you do not want me to marry that awful man."

But the aunt did not smile. Instead her face grew as ugly as Sweaty Hands'.

"Girl," said the aunt in a loud and angry voice, "I will not allow you to speak that way of a man who has given me such fine presents for your worthless self! You will carry the marriage bread to him tomorrow or I'll whip the skin off your back." To prove her point the aunt took a willow switch and brought it down several times across the girl's shoulders until the switch broke. Then, turning her back, the aunt walked away and left Ahweyoh weeping. She did not hear the words which her niece spoke in a soft but determined voice.

"Neh," Ahweyoh said, "I will never marry such a man. First I will die."

That night, when Grandmother Moon looked down from her sky and all others in the village slept, a single small bark canoe left the shores of Cayuga Creek. Her paddle moving with short sure strokes, its lone passenger steered the boat into the rushing waters of the Niagara River. Downstream the rumbling noise of the great falls of Neahga could be heard. Then, as the current swept her faster and faster downstream, Ahweyoh threw away her paddle.

"Forgive me, my parents," she said, raising her hands. "Now I must join you in death. I give myself into the hands of the Thunderers whose voices come from the great falls." Folding her hands in her lap, she sat calmly as the bark canoe rushed downstream, was lifted as if it weighed no more than a drifting leaf and catapulted over the lip of the great falls. She closed her eyes, waiting to be smashed to pieces on the rocks below.

But, instead of striking foaming water and great stones, she felt herself land on something which stopped her fall. She opened her eyes. She was at the base of the falls. In front of her like a great wall of ice flowed the falling water and her face was moist with the mist. She was resting on a big blanket which was held firmly by three men. Ahweyoh looked at them and then looked quickly away. Surely this was a dream. They were dressed in warrior costumes and on the head of each was a single large feather. They were more handsome and strong than any men she had ever seen before.

One warrior was taller than the others. On his back was a pack basket filled with pieces of flint stone. "Little Sister," said the tallest of the men, "we heard you call our name. Often have we watched you from above as you worked without complaining. We have seen how you always give thanks for the fruits of the earth and for the good rain which we send. It was not right that one such as you should end her life in this way."

Ahweyoh could hardly believe her ears. This man was He-noh, the Thunderer and the others were his helpers. These men were the ones who ranged the sky, sending down the rain to help the earth, the ones whose lightning bolts terrified evil-doers and protected the good. Often had she heard it said that the Thunderers lived beneath the great falls, liking the sound of its thunder. Now she knew it was true.

"Nyah-weh," she said, "I thank you for my life."

All three of the men smiled at her. "Come," said the leader. His voice was deep and rumbled like the thunder, yet it was filled with peace. "You shall stay with us now."

So it was that Water Lily came to dwell with the Thunderers. As time went on it became clear that there was love between her and the leader of the Thunderers and the two were married. Things went on happily for them and when the space of four seasons had passed Ahweyoh gave birth to a son.

"Now, my wife," said He-noh, "You must go for a time to live among your own people. Our son must know what it is like to be a human being. When the time is right, you shall return to us again."

"Nyoh," Ahweyoh said. It was right. Though she had been badly treated by the aunt, she longed to see her own people again. Their son should know something of the human world.

"Now listen well," said He-noh. "These are matters of great importance. As you bring up our son you must remember to keep him hidden away. Tell no one who his father is. As he grows, caution him never to grow angry at anyone. As long as he remembers this, he can remain among human beings.

"Now that you are returning to your people, I must tell you why it is that so many have died of sickness. Under your village in a great burrow lives a monstrous snake. This snake eats the bodies of your people after they die and have been buried. It does not come out of the earth for fear we will kill it with our lightning stones. It goes to the places where your people drink and it poisons the waters so they will die in numbers to satisfy its appetite. This it does once a year. Then it sleeps until again it feels hunger. Soon it will wake again. Before it wakens, you must tell your people to move to the Buffalo Creek."

Bearing her husband's words in mind, Ahweyoh returned to her people at Gaugwa. Her face shone like a cloud touched by the sun and her clothing was so fine and beautiful that the people did not recognize her. But Sweaty Hands and the aunt thought this strange woman with a child whose face was covered in its cradleboard looked something like that girl they had lost. To the Clan Mothers Ahweyoh spoke her words of warning with such simple eloquence that they were convinced of the truth. They in turn spoke to the Council of Elders and before three sunrises had come and gone the whole village had moved to Buffalo Creek.

That night the monstrous serpent woke. It crawled through its burrows to poison the springs. Then it waited in a hole beneath the place where the Gaugwa people buried their dead. For the space of a moon it waited, yet no dead bodies were buried. Its hunger grew greater and greater. Finally it pushed its head out of the earth to see what was wrong. Around it was a deserted village.

The monstrous serpent grew angry. How could they dare to move away! Scenting the trail they had taken, it came out of the ground, heedless of danger. It crawled into the lake where their canoes had gone and began to go up Buffalo Creek.

Looking down from a cloud in the sky, He-noh and his warriors saw that the time was right. As the serpent came up the narrow creek, its body filling it from one bank to the other, He-noh hurled a thunder stone. It struck the serpent in its side, making a terrible wound. The monster squirmed and thrashed about, trying to turn around and seek the safety of the deeper water, but the Thunderers struck again and again. To this day the banks of that stream are curved in the spot where the monstrous serpent shoved against its sides.

At last the monster was dead. It began to float downstream and entered the river. Down it floated until it reached the great falls and lodged against the stones, its body stretching across the river like a broken circle. For a time the water was held back. Then a great piece of the falls broke away. That place where the monstrous serpent's body became caught is today called the Horseshoe Falls. As the stones fell, they destroyed the place where the Thunderers had lived. Though the great falls still echo their voices, no longer would He-noh and his helpers dwell beneath the falls. From that day forward, their dwelling place on earth has been far to the west.

Now the people of Gaugwa were happy. They gave great honor to Ahweyoh and built for her a lodge at the edge of the village. She asked to be allowed to live there in seclusion and no one thought of troubling her—except the aunt and Sweaty Hands. The aunt began to spread stories about this woman with a baby and no husband. Sweaty Hands asked again and again why it was that no one was allowed to see the child's face. Most of the people would not listen to such gossip, saying that Hawenio, our Creator, did not like human beings to talk badly about each other, but still the aunt and Sweaty Hands persisted. Seasons came and went. The baby grew to be a small boy crawling about the floor of the lodge, but still no one was allowed to see his face.

Finally, one night, the aunt and Sweaty Hands could stand it no longer. They would go together and confront this woman who so resembled their Ahweyoh of old. If indeed she was that girl, she would be forced to marry Sweaty hands, baby or not!

The aunt brought a willow switch and Sweaty Hands carried a stick which was shaped like a snake. Some of the people in the village saw where they were headed and thought to stop them, but a wise old woman shook her head.

"Neh," she said, "wait a bit. Those who think evil of others usually bring it upon themselves."

When the aunt and Sweaty Hands reached the lodge of Ahweyoh and her son, they paused at the door. A stick had been leaned across the doorway. This meant that those within the lodge did not wish to be disturbed. They paid no attention and pushed their way in. There, in front of a small fire, sat Ahweyoh. Across from her, his back turned to them, her small son sat, playing with some chips of flint.

"Ha-a-ah," said the aunt in her loud angry voice, "now I know you, my niece. You will come with us now and marry this man as I promised." She stepped across the fire and grabbed Ahweyoh by the arm, raising the switch to strike her. Sweaty Hands stepped forward to grab Ahweyoh's other arm, but as he did so he looked for the first time into the face of Ahweyoh's son.

The eyes of the boy caught his attention. At first they were the clear blue of a calm sky, but as they took in the sight of these two people threatening his mother, they became as grey and dark as a thundercloud. With an angry shout the boy hurled the chips of flint in his small hands at the two intruders. Immediately two bolts of lightning struck the aunt and Sweaty Hands. When the smoke cleared, Ahweyoh and her son stood there alone.

From the sky came a great cloud. As it touched the earth He-noh and his two helpers stepped down.

"Now," said He-noh, "it is time for you both to return to us."

And so it was. Ahweyoh and the son of He-noh joined him. From that day there were four Thunderers, for the boy grew up to join his father. At times, though, the Thunder Boy comes down and walks on the earth, remembering the short time when he was a human being. And when storms roll across the sky you can sometimes hear the lightning answer from below as Thunder Boy and his father speak to each other.

Without another word, they handed him the gun.

four
Iroquois hunters

Once, not long ago, four Iroquois hunters spent the winter together trapping in the north. They had good luck. When they brought their furs to the trading post at the end of the season, they had more than enough to buy all the things they needed for their families. In fact, there was just enough left over to buy a new rifle.

They had a problem. Although they hunted and trapped together as brothers, for all of them belonged to the Bear Clan, they did not live together. One hunter was from the Nundawaono, the People of the Great Hill, the Seneca. His home was to the west. One was from the Gueugwehono, the People of the Mucky Land, the Cayuga. His home was to the south near the marshes by the long lakes. One was from the Onundagaono, the People on the Hills, the Onondaga. His place was in the very center of the lands of the Great League. One was from the Ganeagaono, the People of the Flint, the Mohawks. His home was to the east. Now that they had finished trapping, each would be returning home. It was easy to divide provisions among four people, but how could they divide the rifle? Finally it was decided. The man who told the tallest story about hunting would take the gun home.

The Mohawk hunter spoke first. "A man was walking along. He had been hunting all day, but his mind wasn't on his hunting. He'd used up all of the bullets for his old muzzle loader without hitting anything. As he walked, he ate some cherries he had picked. Eat one, spit the stone into his hand. Eat one, spit the stone into his hand. Then he saw, right in front of him, a big, big deer. But he had no bullets left. He thought quickly. He poured powder into the gun, took the cherry seeds, loaded them and fired at the deer's head. The deer fell down, but it got right up again and ran away.

"Some years later that same hunter went out again hunting in the same place. Again he had no luck. Near the end of the day he saw at the edge of a clearing a tall tree covered with ripe cherries. *Ah*, this man thought, *At least I can eat some cherries*. So he put his gun down and began to climb up into the tree. He had reached the lower branches when the tree began to shake back and forth and the hunter had to hold on with both hands. Then the tree lifted straight up into the air and he was thrown out. He looked up from the ground and saw that the tree was growing from between the antlers of a huge deer which shook its head one more time and then ran away into the forest. And that," said the Mohawk hunter, "is my story."

Now it was the turn of the Onondaga hunter. "One time my uncle was out hunting. He had only one shot left in his gun and he wanted to make it count. He came to a stream where he saw a duck swimming back and forth, back and forth. Just in front of the duck there was a large trout and it was leaping from the water to catch flies, leaping, leaping, leaping. On the other side of the stream there stood a deer. It had its head up and it was standing still, sniffing the wind. Further back on a small hill was a bear up on its hind legs, scratching its claws on a tree, up and down, up and down. My uncle got down on his belly. He crawled close to the stream, took careful aim and waited. When everything was just right and the trout jumped again he pulled the trigger. His bullet went through the trout and killed the duck. It ricocheted off the water and struck the deer. It went through the deer and killed the bear. My uncle was a good shot. The amazing thing—I know you will find this hard to believe—is that when he went to skin the bear he turned it over and found it had fallen on a fox and killed it." The Onondaga hunter paused for breath. "And that fox had a fat rabbit in its mouth."

The Cayuga hunter was next. "Many seasons ago my grandfather was out hunting and saw a deer. He started to chase it so he could get closer for a better shot, but he ran so fast he went right past the deer. When the deer saw my grandfather go by him, it got scared. It turned around, jumped as hard as it could and sailed right over a stream. My grandfather jumped too but when he got halfway over the stream he saw he couldn't make it to the other side so he turned around in mid-air and jumped back. By now the deer hid behind a hill on the other side of the stream so my grandfather couldn't see it anymore.

"Now my grandfather was angry. He wasn't going to let that deer get away! He put his gun between two little maple trees and bent the barrel. The he aimed and shot. The bullet curved right around the hill and struck the deer.

"When my grandfather saw the fallen deer he got real excited. It was as if it was the first deer he'd ever shot. He started to skin it right away, but the deer wasn't dead. Just when my grandfather reached the horns and was about to pull the skin off, the deer jumped up and began to run around. My grandfather tried to grab the deer, but it was too slippery. He chased it around and around. Then the skin got caught on the bark of a hickory tree. The deer backed off and pulled real hard and the skin came right off over its horns! The deer ran away, leaving my grandfather with nothing but its skin." The Cayuga hunter looked up and took a deep breath. "And if you don't believe my story, you can just go to my grandfather's lodge. That skin is still hanging there."

Now only the Seneca hunter was left. He looked around at the other three. Then he smiled and shook his head. "Wah-ah," he said, "I am sorry. None of us Senecas ever tell tall stories about hunting."

The other three hunters looked at each other. Then, without another word, they handed him the gun.

"Honh! the Stone Giant roared. "Who is over there? Are you Skunny-Wundy who says he can destroy me?"

Skunny-Wundy
and the
Stone Giant

a long time ago, there lived a person called Skunny-Wundy. He wasn't very big and he wasn't very small, but everybody knew him well because he was always boasting about his bravery. He would talk about all the brave things he had done and all the brave things he was going to do until people would beg him to stop. They weren't quick to do so, however, because Skunny-Wundy, whose name meant Cross-The-Creek, loved only one thing more than he loved to boast: he loved playing tricks on people.

Now in those days there lived some terrible monsters. There were people who could turn themselves into monster bears. And there were great Flying Heads who could destroy whole villages. There were monsters hiding in the springs who grabbed careless travellers, and great horned serpents living in the lakes. But the most frightening monsters of all were the Stone Giants.

The Stone Giants were also called Flint Coats because they had skins harder than stone. If an arrow was aimed at them, it would break on their tough skins. A lance would just bounce off. They were taller than the biggest pine trees and when they walked the earth would shake under their feet. They were very brave: when they boasted, they bragged that they feared no one, not even the Holder Up of the Heavens. But they were also very stupid. The people were very afraid of the Stone Giants for it was well known that their favorite food was human beings.

One day an exhausted runner burst into Skunny-Wundy's village. "The Flint Coats," he gasped, "they are not very far from our town."

Everybody in the town was afraid. People began collecting their belongings so that they could flee for the hills, while grim-faced men prepared their weapons, ready to lay down their lives so that their families could escape.

Skunny-Wundy had just finished eating a big meal and was sleeping in the sun. He was awakened by the noise of people running to and fro. "What is wrong?" he inquired. "Why is everyone running back and forth? The village looks like an anthill after someone has poked a stick into it."

"We are afraid the Stone Giants will find our village and kill us all. Even you must be afraid of the Flint Coats, Skunny-Wundy," a woman said.

"Hah," said Skunny-Wundy, "I am not afraid of anything!"

Everyone in the village stopped and looked at him.

The old sachem was interested. "Aren't you even afraid of the Stone Giants?"

"Hah," said Skunny-Wundy, "I will destroy the Stone Giants if they dare to fight me. There is no greater warrior than Skunny-Wundy. If . . ."

Without his noticing it, everyone crept quietly away and left Skunny-Wundy standing there shaking his stone hatchet and boasting. While he strode up and down, all the people gathered in the Council House. Soon a young man came out and ran out of the village only to return a few minutes later, but Skunny-Wundy did not even notice.

All the people, led by the old sachem, came out of the Council House and gathered around Skunny-Wundy. The old man said, "Skunny-Wundy, rejoice. We have decided to give you a chance to prove your bravery."

Skunny-Wundy stopped striding back and forth. He looked around. All eyes in the village were focused on him. "Ah," he said with a worried look, "that is very good. But . . . uh . . . what do you mean?"

"We have decided," the old man said with just a hint of a smile, "to allow you to fight the Flint Coats."

"Oh," Skunny-Wundy said, "that is good, but . . . how can I find the Stone Giants? Why . . . they might even run away when they see me coming."

"Do not worry," the old man answered, smiling broadly. "A very big Stone Giant stands even now on the other side of the river. He is waiting for you. We sent a messenger to tell him he should run away

163

before the mighty warrior Skunny-Wundy arrived to destroy him. That made the Stone Giant so angry he swore he would stay there until you arrived."

Skunny-Wundy was very frightened, but he knew he had to accept this challenge. If he didn't, people would make fun of him forever.

"Hah," Skunny-Wundy said, "that is good. I shall go now to fight the Flint Coat." He strode quickly out of the village. However, as soon as he was out of sight, he began to walk more slowly. He needed time to think. How could he defeat such a monster?

"If I throw rocks at him," he said to himself, "he'll catch them and chew them up like ripe berries. If I shoot arrows at him, they'll snap like blades of dry grass. No, I must think. Stone Giants aren't very bright after all. Perhaps I can think of some way to trick him."

Just then, Skunny-Wundy heard a very loud, frightening noise that sounded like the beating of a gigantic drum or the roaring of a hurricane wind. It came from the direction of the river just beyond the trees. Skunny-Wundy crept closer. He peered out from behind a tree and saw what he had been afraid he would see.

There on the other side of the river stood the biggest, ugliest, angriest Stone Giant anyone could ever imagine. He had pulled a giant pine tree up by the roots and was beating it against the earth, making a noise like an enormous drum. As he pounded the ground, he sang a terrible war song in a voice as loud as a hurricane.

Skunny-Wundy began to turn around so that he could tiptoe away, but it was too late.

"HONH!" the Stone Giant roared. "WHO IS OVER THERE? ARE YOU SKUNNY-WUNDY WHO SAYS HE CAN DESTROY ME?"

Skunny-Wundy stepped out from behind a tree. "Yes!" he shouted. "I am Skunny-Wundy and it is true that I can destroy you. Come over here and fight me!"

Holding the giant pine tree in one hand like a war club, the Stone Giant waded into the river. The water was deep and before he was halfway across he disappeared under the water. Quick as a fox, Skunny-Wundy hurried upstream where the river was shallow and quickly crossed over to the other side.

Before long, the Stone Giant's head came out of the water near the other side. He climbed up onto the bank where Skunny-Wundy had been standing.

"HONH!" the Stone Giant roared. "WHERE IS SKUNNY-WUNDY?"

"Here I am!" shouted Skunny-Wundy from the other side.

The Stone Giant turned and looked at him. "WHY DID YOU GO OVER THERE?" he growled.

"Over where?" Skunny-Wundy answered. "I'm still waiting for you. You must have gotten turned around under water. If you aren't afraid of me, come over here and fight."

The Stone Giant roared with anger and rushed into the river. He immediately disappeared under the water and Skunny-Wundy had to run quickly to cross over to the other side of the river. He ran so fast he dropped his stone hatchet and left it behind.

When the Stone Giant climbed out of the water

again, there was no sign of Skunny-Wundy, but right in front of him was Skunny-Wundy's hatchet.

"WHAT IS THIS?" growled the Stone Giant. "THIS MUST BE A TOY." He lifted the hatchet to his mouth and touched it to his tongue to test its sharpness. Then he struck Skunny-Wundy's hatchet against a great boulder. To his surprise, the boulder split right in two!

Meanwhile, Skunny-Wundy was watching from the other side of the river. He had heard that any weapon touched by the saliva of a Stone Giant would have magical power and now he knew that it was true. Skunny-Wundy slipped out from behind the trees and waved his arms.

"Hah!" Skunny-Wundy shouted. "Come over here and bring me back my hatchet, so that I can cut off your head with it."

For the first time in his long life, the Stone Giant felt fear in his cold flint heart. If Skunny-Wundy's little stone hatchet could split great boulders in two, Skunny-Wundy would surely be able to destroy him. "No," pleaded the Stone Giant, "do not kill me. You are a terrible warrior. Let me go and I will see that none of my people ever come near your village again."

Skunny-Wundy pretended to think for a minute. Then he nodded his head. "That is good. You may go and save your life. But always remember Skunny-Wundy, the great warrior!"

The Stone Giant hastened away, leaving Skunny-Wundy's hatchet on the river bank. As soon as he was out of sight, Skunny-Wundy crossed over and retrieved his weapon. "Now I must return to my village. My people will be very glad to hear the stories I shall tell them."

Thus it was that Skunny-Wundy used his wits to defeat the Stone Giant and returned to his people, more boastful than ever.

Hodadenon grew smaller and smaller until he was small
enough to travel with the mole under the earth.

hodadenon: the Last One Left and the Chestnut tree

Long ago a boy and his uncle lived together in an elm bark lodge. The boy's name was Hodadenon, which means "The Last One Left." All of the rest of his family had disappeared over the years and it was thought they had been killed by those who were *otgont*, possessed of wicked powers.

Each morning the uncle would feed Hodadenon and then go out of the lodge to hunt, leaving the boy by himself. Each evening he would return, again feed the boy, and then go to sleep.

One day Hodadenon was playing by himself in the lodge. He began to think. "Enh," he said, "why is it that I never see my uncle eat?"

Then he took a bone awl and made a small hole in the deerskin he used as a blanket each night. "Tonight," said Hodadenon, "I shall see what happens after we go to bed."

That evening as always the uncle returned. He fed the boy and told him to go to sleep. Hodadenon lay down on one side of the fire and on the other side the uncle lay down on his couch, which was made of saplings and covered with many animal skins.

Pulling the deerskin over his head, Hodadenon pretended to sleep, but he could still see his uncle through the small hole he had made. After a time, the uncle stood up and went over to the fire.

"Hodadenon," said the uncle in a soft voice, but the boy did not answer. Three times more the uncle called his name, but Hodadenon still pretended to sleep. Coming closer to the fire, the uncle blew very hard into it. Sparks flew out, landing on the boy's legs.

"Hodadenon," said the uncle, "be careful. You are going to be burned." But even though some of the sparks fell on his bare skin and burned him Hodadenon did not move.

"Nyoh," said the uncle, "the boy is indeed asleep." He went over to his couch and removed the skins. He lifted off the top of the couch and took out a box made of birch bark. All of this Hodadenon watched through the hole in his blanket.

Opening the box made of birch bark, the uncle took out a small pot. It was so small that it fit easily in the palm of his hand. From inside the pot he took out another object which the boy could not clearly see though it looked to be smaller than an acorn. Using a little knife, the uncle scraped tiny shavings from the thing into the pot. Then, putting the tiny pot over the fire, he blew on it and sang this song:

Grow, pot, grow in size

Grow, pot, grow in size

And as Hodadenon watched, the pot grew in size as the uncle sang his song and blew on it. Finally the pot was as large as a normal cooking pot and the odor of something delicious came from it. Before long the food was ready and the uncle ate it all. When he was through, he blew once more on the pot and sang this song:

Shrink, pot, shrink in size

Shrink, pot, shrink in size

And once again the pot became small enough to hold in the palm of his hand. Replacing the thing he had scraped in the tiny pot, Hodadenon's uncle replaced the pot in the birch bark box and again hid everything in the secret compartment under his couch. Then he went to sleep.

The next morning, as always, the uncle went out hunting and left the boy alone in the lodge. For a time Hodadenon played around the lodge. He shot his small bow and arrow at a target and did other things, but the song his uncle sang to the pot kept going through his head. Finally he could stand it no longer.

"My uncle will be back soon from his hunting," he said. "He will be very hungry. I should prepare a meal for him."

Hodadenon went over to his uncle's couch, pulled off the skins and opened the compartment. Taking out the box of birch bark, he opened it and found the tiny pot. Within it was half of a small dry nut.

"So this is my uncle's food," said Hodadenon, "but it is almost gone. If I want to make enough for him to eat, I must use it all. I am sure he can get more."

So Hodadenon took a knife and scraped all that was left of the nut into the tiny pot. Then, placing the pot over the fire, he blew on it and sang:

Grow, pot, grow in size
Grow, pot, grow in size

Sure enough, just as it had done for his uncle, the pot became larger. Now it was the size of a normal cooking pot and it was boiling and boiling.

But Hodadenon was not satisfied, "surely my uncle will be more hungry than this when he comes home. I must make more." Then he blew on the pot and again sang:

Grow, pot, grow in size
Grow, pot, grow in size

Now the pot was so large and bubbling so fast that Hodadenon had to stretch to stir the contents, which smelled very good indeed.

"Neh," said Hodadenon, "this isn't enough. What if my uncle wishes to share this good food with me. After all, he will be grateful that I prepared it. I must make more." So, once more, he blew on the kettle and sang the song. Again the pot grew and now it was so large that Hodadenon had to stand on top of his uncle's couch and use a canoe paddle to stir the contents, but he was so excited that he did not want to stop.

"This is almost enough for us," he said, "but what

if we should have visitors? We should have enough to offer them as well."

So, for a fourth time, Hodadenon blew on the pot and sang the magic song. The pot grew so big that Hodadenon had to get out of the lodge because it filled the whole place from side to side! It was so big that the only way the boy could stir it was by taking a long pole up to the roof and reaching down to stir it through the smoke hole!

When Hodadenon's uncle came back from hunting, the first thing he saw was the pudding bubbling out of the door of the lodge. He heard someone singing above him and looked up. There was Hodadenon, swinging his legs in the smoke hole, still stirring the pudding and singing happily:

What a good cook I am
What a good cook I am
We all will eat well now
What a good cook I am

"Nephew," called the old man, "come down from there. What you have done has killed me."

Then Hodadenon's uncle blew on the pot through the door of the lodge and sang the song to make it grow small. When it was down to the size it had been at the beginning, he entered the lodge, lay down on his couch and began to weep.

Hodadenon, who had come down from the smoke hole, walked over to where the old man lay.

"Uncle," said Hodadenon, "what is wrong?"

"Hodadenon," said the uncle, "you have used up all of the only food I can eat. Now I will starve to death. This is why I never allowed you to see me eat. I knew that you would do this."

"Uncle," said the boy, "things can't be that bad. Just go and get another of those little nuts."

"Neh," said the uncle, "that is the kind of food called a chestnut. Long ago, though it was very dangerous, I obtained that one. All these years I have eaten it and it would have lasted for many more. Now I am too old to get another one."

"Wah-ah," said Hodadenon, "this is my doing. I shall go and bring back many chestnuts."

"It is not possible," said the old man. "The way is long and guarded by many terrible creatures. Others of your family have gone there but none have ever returned."

Yet Hodadenon would not give up. Finally the uncle agreed to tell him the way. "Go straight to the north," the uncle said. "There you will find a narrow path. At its first turn it is guarded by two great rattlesnakes, slaves to the evil ones who own the chestnut trees. No one can get past them."

"But what if I do, Uncle?" asked Hodadenon.

"If anyone by good luck passes the great snakes, he will next encounter two huge bears. They guard a passageway between the rocks. They too are slaves of the evil ones. They will tear apart anyone who tries to pass.

"Further on down the path are two giant Panthers which leap upon anyone who attempts to get by them. Hodadenon, it cannot be done."

"Is that all, Uncle?" Hodadenon said.

"Is it not enough?" said the old man. "Neh, that is only the beginning. Next is the place where the chestnut trees grow. There live the seven sisters who own the trees. All of them are strong in *otgont* power. If anyone comes to steal the chestnuts, they run from their long lodge and beat the person to death with their clubs. No one can hope to go undetected, for a flayed human skin hangs in the top of a tree looking down on the chestnut grove and it sings a warning when anyone comes close."

"Nyah-weh, Uncle," said Hodadenon, "I thank you for your good advice. Now I must be on my way. I shall return with the food you need if all goes well."

Taking two sticks, he tied them together and placed them standing near the fire. "Watch these sticks, Uncle," said the boy. "If all is well with me they will not move, but if I am killed they will break apart."

Now Hodadenon set out on his way. He went straight to the north and found a narrow path. "This must be the road my uncle told me of," said Hodadenon. "It looks easy enough to travel."

The boy continued along and soon the path began to twist and wind. Ahead, it turned sharply to the left. Hodadenon stopped, crept off the path, went through the trees, and peered out cautiously. There, on either side of the path, were two great rattlesnakes, coiled and ready to strike.

"Uncle," said Hodadenon, "you know this road well." He went and caught two chipmunks. Holding one in each hand he again began to walk the path.

When he came to the two rattlesnakes he threw a chipmunk into the mouth of each before they could strike him.

"Tca," he said, "you seem to be in need of food. Now I have given you that which you should hunt for yourselves. Hawenio, our Creator, did not make any of his beings to be slaves. Go from this place."

As soon as he finished speaking, the two rattlesnakes uncoiled and crawled off in different directions, leaving the road unguarded as Hodadenon went along his way.

Meanwhile, back at the lodge, the two tied sticks which had been quivering now stood still as Hodadenon's uncle watched them intently.

Now the path entered a rocky place. Again Hodadenon left the trail to scout ahead. There, where the way dipped between two big boulders, were a pair of giant bears, crouched and ready to tear apart anybody who tried to go by.

"Uncle," said Hodadenon, "you have travelled this road before." He climbed a tree where he heard the buzzing of many bees, pulled out two combs of honey and went back onto the path. When he came to the bears, he hurled the combs of honey into their mouths before they could grab him.

"Hunh," the boy said, "it looks to me as if you were hungry. Now I have given you that which you like best of all. The one who gave us breath, Hawenio, did not make us to be the slaves of anyone. Go from this place."

At his words, the two bears turned and went away,

each in a different direction as Hodadenon continued down the trail.

Meanwhile, back at the uncle's lodge, the two tied sticks stopped quivering and Hodadenon's uncle breathed a sigh of relief.

Now the path entered a deep forest and wound between large trees. Leaving the trail, Hodadenon crept along till he could see the place where two huge panthers, eyes glowing like green flames, hid behind a pair of giant pines on either side of the path.

"Uncle," Hodadenon said, "you remember your travels well." Taking his bow and arrows, he killed two deer. Carrying them over his shoulders, he went down the trail once more. Before the panthers could leap upon him, he threw each of them a deer.

"Ee-yah," he said, "I see that you were in need of food. Now I have given you that which you are supposed to hunt. Know that the one who gave us strength to walk around, Hawenio, did not intend that any living creature should serve another as a slave. Go from this place."

In two different directions away into the trees slunk the panthers and the boy continued along his way.

Meanwhile, back at the lodge, the two sticks which had been shaking as if struck by a strong wind once more stood still as Hodadenon's uncle watched them.

The path in front of Hodadenon was very straight and wide. It looked to have been travelled by many feet. The boy listened very carefully and soon he began to hear a very faint song coming from the treetops. Crawling forward through the brush, he peered up and saw the one who was singing. It was the skin of a woman tied in the top of a tree. This was her song:

Gi-nu, gi-nu, gi-nu
I am the one who sees all,
I see you

The song was very soft. Hodadenon could barely hear it, but he knew it would grow loud indeed if she caught a glimpse of him. Below her was a grove of trees. They were covered with a fruit which had burrs all over it. These, Hodadenon knew, must be the chestnuts. Beyond the skin woman and the trees was a great pile of human bones and just to the other side of them was the long lodge of the seven witches.

"Tcu," said Hodadenon, "now I shall need some help." Going to a basswood tree, he peeled a long strip of bark. With a burned stick and the juice of berries, he decorated the piece of bark until it looked just like a long wampum belt. Slinging it over his shoulder, he knelt down and tapped four times on the earth.

"My friend," he said, "I am in need of help."

Up out of the ground poked the nose and then the head of a female mole.

"Nyoh, Hodadenon! How can I help you?" asked the mole.

"Grandmother," said the boy, "if I make myself very small, will you carry me under the earth with

178

you?"

"That's too easy," said the mole. "Let's go!"

Then Hodadenon began to rub himself with his hands. As he did so he grew smaller and smaller until he was small enough to travel with the mole under the earth. Down into the ground they went, coming up beneath the very tree where the Skin Woman was swaying back and forth. Once again Hodadenon rubbed himself with his hands until he was back to normal. Then he called up to Skin Woman.

"Sister," he called, "I have seen you first. Do not tell the others I am here and I will give you this fine belt of wampum."

"Wah-ah!" said Skin Woman, "I did not see you, Hodadenon. Give me the belt and I will not warn them you are here."

Hodadenon tossed the belt up to Skin Woman. She put it on and immediately it wrapped itself so tightly about her she could not speak. Under the tree, Hodadenon quickly filled his pouch with chestnuts. Then, making himself small once more, he called for his friend, Mole, to take him back under the earth.

Up in the tree, Skin Woman finally got her breath. She began to sing:

Gi-nu, gi-nu, gi-nu
Someone has bribed me
I cannot say who

Out from the long lodge ran the seven witches. Each of them carried a long club. They ran to the place where Skin Woman hung, but they saw no one.

"Someone has been here," said one of the witches.

"Some of our chestnuts are gone," said another.

"Skin Woman," said a third witch, "you are our slave. Speak and tell us who has been here."

But Skin Woman did not answer the question. All she did was swing back and forth in the wind, singing this song:

Gi-nu, gi-nu, gi-nu
I've been given a wampum belt
Shining and new

"You are a fool," said another of the witches. "That is only the bark from a tree."

"It must have been The Last One Left," said the fifth witch, "the boy whose uncle stole from us long ago."

"If he comes back," said the sixth witch, "we will catch him and kill him."

"Nyoh," said the last witch, "now we must punish our slave." She took her club and struck Skin Woman a heavy blow. Each of the others did the same. Then the seven witches went back into the long lodge, leaving the Skin Woman covered with bruises, but still singing softly of her fine new belt of wampum.

Meanwhile, back in the lodge of Hodadenon's uncle, the two sticks had fallen over on the floor. Picking them up and standing them upright once more, the old man watched them with great concern.

From his hiding place in the earth, Hodadenon had listened to all that was said by the seven sisters.

"It is not right," he said, "that those terrible creatures should go on like this. Friend Mole, we must go back there."

The mole dove deeper into the earth. She carried Hodadenon under the long lodge and came up beneath the couch where the sisters slept. There, tied to a string of sinew, were seven hearts. Quick as a spark leaping from the fire, Hodadenon grabbed the string of hearts and ran from the lodge. Seeing him, the seven witches grabbed their clubs and gave chase.

Now back in the lodge of Hodadenon's uncle the two sticks fell over once more. The old man was so disheartened that he did not stand them up again. He lay there staring at them, certain that his nephew would now never return alive.

From the top of her tree, Skin Woman sang as the seven witches chased Hodadenon:

Gi-nu, gi-nu, gi-nu
Hodadenon has your hearts
This will be the end of you

Now the first witch had almost caught up with the boy and raised her club to strike him. As she did so, Hodadenon squeezed one of the hearts on the sinew string and the witch fell dead. Now the second witch was about to strike. Again Hodadenon squeezed a heart and the second witch died also. In the end, he had squeezed all seven of the hearts and all seven of the evil sisters had fallen dead.

Climbing to the top of the tree, Hodadenon cut loose the cords which held Skin Woman. He brought her down and placed her on top of the pile of human bones. Then he began to push against a great dead hickory tree which was near the pile.

"Get yourselves up, my relatives!" he shouted. "A tree is about to fall on you!"

Immediately Skin Woman and all of the people whose bones were piled there leaped up and came back to life. Skin Woman was, indeed, the sister of Hodadenon. Long ago the evil witches had caught her and the others of his family whose bones lay in that pile. There before him were his parents, his brothers, and all his relations. All were very happy to be alive and thanked the boy again and again.

Taking the chestnuts from the ground, Hodadenon passed them out to all his relatives.

"Plant these all over," he said. "Food will be shared with everyone from now on."

Finally, his pouch filled with chestnuts, Hodadenon went back to the lodge of his uncle. The old man lay there on his couch, thin as a skeleton, his eyes fixed on the two tied sticks.

"Uncle," said Hodadenon, "I have returned."

The old man jumped up and embraced the nephew. To this day he still sits in that lodge, making chestnut pudding in his pot. And from that time on, the chestnuts, like all the other good things given to us by Hawenio, our Creator, no longer belong to just one family, no matter how powerful they are, but are shared by all.

The flying head swept through the forest following her trail.

the Brave Woman and the flying head

There was once a woman who travelled to a nearby village, her infant son strapped to a cradleboard on her back. She was bringing food to her relatives whose crops had not done well that season.

When she was deep in the forest, she heard a terrible sound, the sound of trees being knocked down, the sound of a great wind coming in her direction. She looked back and there, far away, above the tree tops, was a Flying Head.

Flying Heads were awful creatures, heads with no bodies—just long trailing hair and great paws like those of a bear. Those paws were forever grasping at anything within their reach for the monsters were always hungry.

The woman knew the Flying Head would soon catch her scent and so she quickly took the food from her pack and scattered it in every direction. She then began to run. "Have courage," she whispered to her child. "I will not let this monster catch us."

Soon, just as the woman thought, the Flying Head caught the human scent. It swept through the forest following her trail until it came to the scattered food. There it stopped and began to eat, not willing to let even a single crumb escape its hungry mouth.

By the time it finished the last of the food, the woman was far down the path, but the Flying Head was swift as the wind and soon took up the chase. Looking back over her shoulder as she ran, the woman saw the Flying Head close behind her, reaching out its big paws to grab her.

This woman had once heard a wise person say that the moccasin of a tiny child holds great power for good. So, quick as a wink, she tossed one of her son's small shoes behind her into the monster's path.

The Flying Head grabbed with one big paw as the tiny moccasin fell but missed, tangling its long hair in the brush which grew beside the path. Growling, it rolled into a patch of brambles where its long hair was caught. Meanwhile, the woman, running swift as a fox, continued down the path until she could run no further. Then she climbed up high into a tall white pine. "Be silent, my son," she whispered. "The monster will not find us here."

It was not long before the Flying Head untangled itself from the brambles. With a terrible roar it flew into the air following the woman's trail through the forest. Soon it came to the foot of the tree and sniffed about, confused because the human scent went no further.

Just then, high up in the top of the tree, the

185

woman's small son reached out one hand and knocked loose a tiny branch which fell down, down, down . . . and struck the Flying Head. "HAARNNH!" roared the Flying Head. "A porcupine dropped its quills on me!" In anger it struck the tree a blow which knocked loose a huge dead limb that fell right on the Flying Head and pinned it to the ground. While the monster struggled to get free, the woman climbed down from the pine tree and dashed off into the woods.

Now the woman's home was not far away and she ran and ran and ran and ran. Soon she reached the edge of her village and before her was the door of her lodge. She burst inside and fell down by the coals which still glowed from her cooking fire.

For a time she rested, feeling safe at last. Then, thinking that her child might be hungry, she looked around for something to eat. All that was left was a handful of chestnuts which she thrust into the fire to cook.

Meanwhile, the terrible Flying Head freed itself at last from the fallen limb. Filled with rage, it followed the trail of the woman right to the door of her lodge. It flew up and looked down through the smoke hole, ready to swoop in and grab her.

But when it looked down, what did the Flying Head see? It saw the woman reach into the fire, draw something out which looked to be a burning coal and thrust it into her mouth.

"Haarnnh," growled the monster. "She is eating fire. So fire is something good to eat!" It dove down right through the smoke hole and with both paws grabbed all the coals and shoved them deep into its mouth.

"Huunhhh?" it snarled as the fire started to burn within its belly.

"HAAARRRNH!" it screamed as it flew out the smoke hole and was gone.

From that day on, the village of the woman who was brave and did not lose her courage was never again bothered by the Flying Head.

Just as the great bear turned, the fattest and laziest hunter leveled his spear.

the hunting
of the
Great Bear

There were four hunters who were brothers. No hunters were as good as they at following a trail. They never gave up once they began tracking their quarry.

One day, in the moon when the cold nights return, an urgent message came to the village of the four hunters. A great bear, one so large and powerful that many thought it must be some kind of monster, had appeared. The people of the village whose hunting grounds the monster had invaded were afraid. The children no longer went out to play in the woods. The longhouses of the village were guarded each night by men with weapons who stood by the entrances. Each morning, when the people went outside, they found the huge tracks of the bear in the midst of their village. They knew that soon it would become even more bold.

Picking up their spears and calling to their small dog, the four hunters set forth for that village, which was not far away. As they came closer they noticed

189

how quiet the woods were. There were no signs of rabbits or deer and even the birds were silent. On a great pine tree they found the scars where the great bear had reared up on hind legs and made deep scratches to mark its territory. The tallest of the brothers tried to touch the highest of the scratch marks with the tip of his spear.

"It is as the people feared," the first brother said. "This one we are to hunt is Nyah-gwaheh, a monster bear."

"But what about the magic that the Nyah-gwaheh has?" said the second brother.

The first brother shook his head. "That magic will do it no good if we find its track."

"That's so," said the third brother. "I have always heard that from the old people. Those creatures can only chase a hunter who has not yet found its trail. When you find the track of the Nyah-gwaheh and begin to chase it, then it must run from you."

"Brothers," said the fourth hunter who was the fattest and laziest, "did we bring along enough food to eat? It may take a long time to catch this big bear. I'm feeling hungry."

Before long, the four hunters and their small dog reached the village. It was a sad sight to see. There was no fire burning in the center of the village and the doors of all the longhouses were closed. Grim men stood on guard with clubs and spears and there was no game hung from the racks or skins stretched for tanning. The people looked hungry.

The elder sachem of the village came out and the

tallest of the four hunters spoke to him.

"Uncle," the hunter said, "we have come to help you get rid of the monster."

Then the fattest and laziest of the four brothers spoke. "Uncle," he said, "is there some food we can eat? Can we find a place to rest before we start chasing this big bear. I'm tired."

The first hunter shook his head and smiled. "My brother is only joking, Uncle," he said. "We are going now to pick up the monster bear's trail."

"I am not sure you can do that, Nephews," the elder sachem said. "Though we find tracks closer and closer to the doors of our lodges each morning, whenever we try to follow those tracks they disappear."

The second hunter knelt down and patted the head of their small dog. "Uncle," he said, "that is because they do not have a dog such as ours." He pointed to the two black circles above the eyes of the small dog. "Four-Eyes can see any tracks, even those many days old."

"May Creator's protection be with you," said the elder sachem.

"Do not worry, Uncle," said the third hunter. "Once we are on a trail we never stop following it until we've finished our hunt."

"That's why I think we should have something to eat first," said the fourth hunter, but his brothers did not listen. They nodded to the elder sachem and began to leave. Sighing, the fattest and laziest of the brothers lifted up his long spear and trudged after them.

They walked, following their little dog. It kept lifting up its head, as if to look around with its four eyes. The trail was not easy to find.

"Brothers," the fattest and laziest hunter complained, "don't you think we should rest. We've been walking a *long* time." But his brothers paid no attention to him. Though they could see no tracks, they could feel the presence of the Nyah-gwaheh. They knew that if they did not soon find its trail, it would make its way behind them. Then they would be the hunted ones.

The fattest and laziest brother took out his pemmican pouch. At least he could eat while they walked along. He opened the pouch and shook out the food he had prepared so carefully by pounding together strips of meat and berries with maple sugar and then drying them in the sun. But instead of pemmican, pale squirming things fell out into his hands. The magic of the Nyah-gwaheh had changed the food into worms.

"Brothers," the fattest and laziest of the hunters shouted, "let's hurry up and catch that big bear! Look what it did to my pemmican. Now I'm getting angry."

Meanwhile, like a pale giant shadow, the Nyah-gwaheh was moving through the trees close to the hunters. Its mouth was open as it watched them and its huge teeth shone, its eyes flashed red. Soon it would be behind them and on their trail.

Just then, though, the little dog lifted its head and

yelped. "Eh-heh!" the first brother called.

"Four-Eyes has found the trail," shouted the second brother.

"We have the track of the Nyah-gwaheh," said the third brother.

"Big Bear," the fattest and laziest one yelled, "we are after you, now!"

Fear filled the heart of the great bear for the first time and it began to run. As it broke from the cover of the pines, the four hunters saw it, a gigantic white shape, so pale as to appear almost naked. With loud hunting cries, they began to run after it. The great bear's strides were long and it ran more swiftly than a deer. The four hunters and their little dog were swift also though and they did not fall behind. The trail led through the swamps and the thickets. It was easy to read, for the bear pushed everything aside as it ran, even knocking down big trees. On and on they ran, over hills and through valleys. They came to the slope of a mountain and followed the trail higher and higher, every now and then catching a glimpse of their quarry over the next rise.

Now though the lazy hunter was getting tired of running. He pretended to fall and twist his ankle.

"Brothers," he called, "I have sprained my ankle. You must carry me."

So his three brothers did as he asked, two of them carrying him by turns while the third hunter carried his spear. They ran more slowly now because of their heavy load, but they were not falling any further behind. The day had turned now into night, yet they could still see the white shape of the great bear ahead of them. They were at the top of the mountain now and the ground beneath them was very dark as they ran across it. The bear was tiring, but so were they. It was not easy to carry their fat and lazy brother. The little dog, Four-Eyes, was close behind the great bear, nipping at its tail as it ran.

"Brothers," said the fattest and laziest one, "put me down now. I think my leg has gotten better."

The brothers did as he asked. Fresh and rested, the fattest and laziest one grabbed his spear and dashed ahead of the others. Just as the great bear turned to bite at the little dog, the fattest and laziest hunter leveled his spear and thrust it into the heart of the Nyah-Gwaheh. The monster bear fell dead.

By the time the other brothers caught up, the fattest and laziest hunter had already built a fire and was cutting up the big bear.

"Come on, brothers," he said. "Let's eat. All this running has made me hungry!"

So they cooked the meat of the great bear and its fat sizzled as it dripped from their fire. They ate until even the fattest and laziest one was satisfied and leaned back in contentment. Just then, though, the first hunter looked down at his feet.

"Brothers," he exclaimed, "look below us!"

The four hunters looked down. Below them were thousands of small sparkling lights in the darkness which, they realized, was all around them.

"We aren't on a mountain top at all," said the third brother. "We are up in the sky."

And it was so. The great bear had indeed been magical. Its feet had taken it high above the earth as it tried to escape the four hunters. However, their determination not to give up the chase had carried them up that strange trail.

Just then their little dog yipped twice.

"The great bear!" said the second hunter. "Look!"

The hunters looked. There, where they had piled the bones of their feast the Great Bear was coming back to life and rising to its feet. As they watched, it began to run again, the small dog close on its heels.

"Follow me," shouted the first brother. Grabbing up their spears, the four hunters again began to chase the great bear across the skies.

So it was, the old people say, and so it still is. Each autumn the hunters chase the great bear across the skies and kill it. Then, as they cut it up for their meal, the blood falls down from the heavens and colors the leaves of the maple trees scarlet. They cook the bear and the fat dripping from their fires turns the grass white.

If you look carefully into the skies as the seasons change, you can read that story. The great bear is the square shape some call the bowl of the Big Dipper. The hunters and their small dog (which you can just barely see) are close behind, the dipper's handle. When autumn comes and that constellation turns upside down, the old people say, "Ah, the lazy hunter has killed the bear." But as the moons pass and the sky moves once more towards spring, the bear slowly rises back on its feet and the chase begins again.

"Naho," the storyteller says, "I have spoken."

naho

There is silence as the last story ends. The storyteller looks around the circle. "Hoh?" he says, but there is no response. Outside the longhouse the moon, our grandmother, casts her quiet light on the snow. Somewhere in the distance, our clan brother, Wolf, who taught the people to come together in counsel and join their voices in song many ages ago, calls across the hills. The voice of the owl whootooluls, "It is time to sleep."

"Ah," asks the storyteller, "my audience is asleep?" A small child tries to answer just one more time but her words turn instead into a yawn as she settles back into her mother's arms and closes her eyes. Parents and elders smile, remembering when they too struggled to stay awake all night to hear these stories told by old men and women who no longer walk among the living. But their voices and stories are still alive, alive as dreams and magic, courage and faith, alive as the people of the longhouse.

But it is time to sleep and so the parents and the elders nod their thanks to the storyteller.

"Naho," he says, "I have spoken." And he watches his audience slip away to the sleeping quarters which line both sides of the great longhouse. For a time he sits alone by the fire, reading its messages. Then one of his own daughter's children, herself a young woman, comes to him. "Grandfather," she says, "my mother says it is time to rest."

The storyteller smiles. "For tonight," he says, "only for tonight."

Glossary

Ahweyoh: Water Lily.

Dah-joh: Come in or enter. Spoken when someone comes to the door.

Dah-neh hoh: It is finished. Said at the end of a story.

Enh: An exclamation used to indicate a question.

Gayei Nadehogo 'eda': Four-eyed one. Used to describe a dog with a spot over each eye. Such dogs are regarded as magically endowed or very lucky.

Go-weh: A cry indicating distress or danger.

Gustoweh: The Iroquois head-dress. Each of the 5 Nations has its own style, but it consists of a cap with from one to three feathers attached at the top, often in such a fashion as to allow the feather to move or rotate with the wind.

Ha-a-ah: An exclamation of disparagement, belittling someone.

Hageota: A Story Teller.

Hahskwahot: Large standing rock.

Hatho: The Frost Spirit. Usually pictured as an old man in white who carries a large club to strike against the trees.

Hawenio: The Creator.

He-noh: The Thunder Spirit.

Hodadenon: The last one left.

Honh: An expression of challenge.

Hotinonsonni (also *Hau-de-nau-sau-nee*): People of the Long House, The Iroquois, The Six Nations.
These are the:
Nundawaono, The People of the Great Hill (Seneca)
Gueugwehonono, The Mucky Land People (Cayuga)
Onundagaono, The People on the Hills (Onondaga)
Onayotakaono, The Granite or Standing Stone People (Oneida)
Ganeagaono, The Flint People (Mohawk)
Dusgaoweh, Shirt-wearing People (Tuscarora)

Hunh-uh (or *Enh*): An expression of confusion or bewilderment.

Jo-eh-gah: The Raccoon.

Jo-Ge-Oh: The Little People of the Iroquois. Sometimes called "The Jungies." Various families of them are found in caves, in certain desolate ravines, even under water. They have magical powers and are also known as "stone-throwers" because they are very accurate at hurling stones to drive people away. They supposedly keep certain dangerous evil animals penned up underground.

Kweh (or *Noh-kweh*): An expression of sudden excitement.

Neahga: Niagara Falls.

Neh: No.

Nyah-gwaheh: A monster which can take the shape of a human or a large bear.

Nyah-weh: Thank you.

Nyoh: Yes.

Ongwe Ias: The man-eater, the one who eats you. Can be used to describe a cannibal monster or by one animal with reference to another which hunts it as prey.

Skunny-Wundy (or *Skunniwundi*): Name of an Iroquois trickster hero. Means "Cross the Creek" or "At the Rapids."

Wah-ah: An exclamation of regret.

Weh-yoh: An exclamation of joy.

About the Illustrator

Daniel Burgevin was educated at the Chicago Art Institute. He has been active with environmental organizations such as Greenpeace, helping the whales to survive. He considers illustrating these Iroquois stories a rare privilege since he shares the Native American attitude toward the earth, wishing to protect it from greed. He says, "I hope my interpretations show my respect and reverence for these people and their rich history."

David C. Burgevin

about the author

I was born in 1942 in Saratoga Springs in October, the Moon of Falling Leaves. I'm of mixed-blood ancestry, Slovak on my father's side and English and Abenaki Indian on my mother's. I was raised in the small Adirondack foothills town of Greenfield Center in a house built by my maternal grandfather. Aside from attending Cornell University and Syracuse and 3 years of teaching in West Africa, I have spent all my life in Greenfield Center. My wife, Carol, our two teenage sons, Jim and Jesse, and I live in that same house today.

I write poetry, and fiction and I have won national awards for my writing. Some of my poems are included in textbooks used in high schools and junior high. My poems have appeared in more than 400 magazines in the U.S., Canada, England and Africa and I'm the author of 20 published books and chapbooks of poetry and fiction. In recent years I have done more and more story-telling, focussing in particular on the traditional tales of the Abenaki and the Iroquois people of the northeast and the tall tales and logging stories of the Adirondack mountains. Two earlier collections of my retellings of Iroquois folk stories have been published: *Turkey Brother* and *Stone Giants and Flying Heads*, both from The Crossing Press.

I believe that stories are as much a part of human beings as is breath—and that, like breath, stories link us to all other living things and are meant to be shared.

Joseph Bruchac
Gah-neh-goh-he-yoh
Maple Sugar Moon 1985

Bob Mayette